JERUSALEM
SNAPSHOTS FROM A DISTANCE

You shall see and your heart shall rejoice; your bones shall flourish like the grass.

COVER PAGE: QUOTATION FROM ISAIAH INSCRIBED ON ONE OF THE STONES OF THE TEMPLE MOUNT WALL:

JERUSALEM BIRDVIEW

JERUSALEM

SNAPSHOTS FROM A DISTANCE

STORIES BY ESTHER A. DAGAN

JERUSALEM EMBLEM

Amrad Publications
1236 FORT ST. MONTRÉAL, QC, H3H 2B3, CANADA
TEL./FAX: (514)931-4747

Dépôt légal, Bibliothèque Nationale du Québec and
The National Library of Canada, 1st quarter 2003.

Canadian Cataloguing in Publication Data

Dagan, Esther A.
Jerusalem, Snapshots from a Distance
ISBN 1-896371-03-5
1. Short Stories, Canadian (English). 2. Jerusalem 3. Israel
4. Judaism 5. Fiction 6. Palestinian

PS8557.A285J47 2002   C813'.6
C2002-904027-2   PR9199.4.D34J47 2002

Editing and Typesetting by Kimberlie M. Robert
Design and Cover Page by Diane Leyland
Illustrations by Diane Leyland
Printed in Canada by AGMV Marquis

Amrad Publications, previously GAAAP (Galerie Amrad
African Art Publications) has published, since 1985, 14 titles, on
African arts. Changing to **Amrad Publications** in 2002 allows
us to expand our horizons. Our first short story collection: *Mask*,
was the first under our new name. This volume of short stories,
Jerusalem, Snapshots from a Distance, is our second.

Amrad Publications
1236 Fort St. Montréal, QC, H3H 2B3, Canada
Tel./Fax: (514)931-4747

To Halit, who left behind
blessed memories and moments sublime.

*

To the many Ilanot
yet to be born
in the spirit
of Ilan Ramon.

About the author

Born in Jerusalem. Prior to her immigration to Canada in 1978, Esther A. Dagan taught, between '62 and '78, African art and rituals in numerous universities in Israel. Over one hundred of her articles, stories and essays have been published during that period in many Israeli newspapers and magazines. She graduated from a dance academy in Paris and received her B.A. and M.A. in theatre and drama from Tel Aviv University. Her long-lasting interest in African dance and rituals took her to most sub-Saharan countries.

In Canada, to her credit, she authored ten books, edited three, and produced a 58mm video on African dance, all listed at Amazon.com. In recent years, Esther A. Dagan shifted her writing to fictional short stories.

"Terra-Gay," the last story in E.A. Dagan's previous collection *Mask*, published in 2002, won the First Prize for short stories in a contest by The Canadian Authors' Association in 2001. Her story "Beckett? Qui-est-ce?," was published in *(Ex)Cite, Journal of Contemporary Writing*, in November 2001. *Jerusalem, Snapshots from a Distance* is her second collection.

CONTENTS

A 19TH-CENTURY ETCHING OF DAVID TOWER AND THE
CITADEL IN THE TURKISH ERA

Old Jerusalem: Souk Snapshots

Edbach-el-yahud!!!
 Jihad fundamentalist: Hebron, 1929: Hebron, 2002.

Krist-Tall-Nacht!!! Kill the Jews!!!
 Bloodstained, glass explosion: Berlin, 1938.

Kill them!! Throw them in the sea!!
 Mobs: Cairo, Amman, Damascus, Baghdad,
 Beirut, Riad, Tripoli. 1948 to 2002.

Inukjuak, hi! Inukjuak, hi hi! Inukjuak, hi hi hi!!
 Crowd cheering: Nunavit, Canada, 1999.

Hatsilu! Ezraa-aa-aa-aa!!! Allah-Rahim!!!
 Agonised mother's cry: Israel, West Bank, 2002.

Aaabaa!!! Aaabii!!! Imaa!!! Immii!!!
 Children's cries: Israel, West Bank, 2002.

Revenge for our occupation!!!
 Angelic faced, Hamas teenage girl on TV before
 committing suicide and becoming a martyr. 2002.

Israel has no right to exist! It's our land!
 Hizballah, Hamas, El-Aksa-brigades, Islamic Jihad
 suicide bombers, hidden behind masks of Israeli soldiers,
 pregnant woman, Hasidic Jews, blond hippies before blowing
 themselves up in pizzerias, discos, wedding halls, Passover
 celebrations, and on, and on, and on, killing the innocent:
 Israel, 2002.

* * *

S he wakes up. Sweating. Disoriented. Confused in darkness. Where is she? When? Is she in Berlin? The Holy Land? Old Jerusalem? Or is she playing in Inukjuak at the Arctic Summer Games? The games she saw on TV, where the Nunavut celebrated their newly recognized territory? She is not in any of those places. She is in the middle: tormented, in between. She is in Montreal, and the geographical distance is hard to bear.

The recent news from bleeding Israel and the West Bank keeps haunting her. Perhaps it's time to return to Israel, her homeland, to be with her people, to share their agony, frustration and pain—the pain of hope lost.

The daily accumulating painful tension needs to be tunnelled off. Tunnelled to where? Perhaps regression will help—to the good old days—to recapture a fast fading, fond childhood memory.

Unlike the stories told by her grandfather that always began with: "Once upon an old biblical time," her story begins here and now. She invites you, the reader, to join her as a guest on a childhood journey to the souks of the ancient city of Jerusalem where she was born. To make you feel like an old family friend, she would like to introduce herself and her family as they engraved themselves in her memory of 1936.

* * *

I am almost six years old. My name is Simha. In Hebrew, it means joy. This name was given to me by my mother, because I am the firstborn. She always calls me Simhati, my joy. My father accepted this name for a different reason. He wanted his firstborn to be a boy. Unfortunately, I am a girl, but as Simha is a name suited to both boys and girls, it suits my father too.

My father, in Hebrew I call him *Abaa*. He has a coffee shop outside the Old City walls, just below the Jaffa Gate, in the Mamila market. My abaa works very hard with Suleman, his helper. Every day from sunrise to sunset, they make *chai* and *ahowa* for people in the Mamila market. Usually Suleman prepares the coffee and tea and my abaa brings them to the customers on a shiny, round, ornate brass tray with three holders topped with a round handle.

Everyone loves my abaa. He has many names. His Jewish friends call him Moshe; his Muslim friends call him Musa; the Armenians call him Moise; and the Christians call him Moses. My mother? It depends. When she is in a good mood, she calls him Moshi! When she is angry, she calls him Mo-shiii! But, when she is very very angry, she makes the shi much longer, like this: Mo-shiiiiiiiiiiiiiiiiiiiiiiiii! My grandfather, who told me the story about how Moses crossed the sea and saved his people from the Egyptians, likes shortening the names of everyone. He calls my father just Mosh.

My mother's name is Ahuva. In Hebrew, it means the beloved. I call her Ima. My father, when he is cheerful calls her Ahuvati, meaning my love. She takes good care of our family, but what she really loves to do is embroidery. Everything in our home: curtains, sheets, pillowcases, tablecloths and even our clothing are made beautiful with her own hands. I love those peaceful hours when she sits in the shade of the grapevines on our roof with her embroidery. Sometimes, she sings. Often she tells me stories about her childhood, or teaches me the different types of stitches. I already know *Tslavim*, like crosses, and *Sharsheret*, like chains. Soon she will teach me to crochet.

Now that you know *everything* about my family, let's start our journey.

Today is Friday, early morning. It is a hot autumn day in

the Jewish Quarter. Me and my ima are standing beside the courtyard that leads to our home, waiting for you, our guest.

I am neatly dressed in a white embroidered blouse, a navy-blue pleated skirt, white socks, and shiny red shoes. My long black hair, braided by my ima this morning, is tied with red silk ribbons in large butterfly bows. I love butterfly bows. In my left hand is *tike-haochel*, my lunch box. In it is a pita sandwich with feta cheese, olives and fresh cucumber, wrapped in a *mapit*, an embroidered cloth.

Here you are. My ima makes you promise to protect me and never let my hand go until we reach the kindergarten. So, my right hand is secured in yours and your camera, with its large extended shiny eye, hangs around your neck.

They began to walk. Standing atop of round grey stone minarets, Muezzins sang Saalat-El-Fagar, announcing the morning prayers into loud speakers. Under the arched blue sky, a flock of white storks speared the air with their long, red beaks, heading south. The raising sun washed the white stone houses in light shades of pinkish gold. The rays softly brushed strokes of dark golden tones over the domes and towers of the surrounding mosques, churches and synagogues. The mountain, facing the East sidewall, was dotted with vertical tombstones and olive trees. The lower half of the tombstones sank in shadows, while the upper half, dressed with sun, rose in prayer.

"What is that strange looking mountain?"

"That mountain behind the eastern wall is the Mount of Olives, where my grandfather is buried."

"I've never been to Jerusalem. I wonder if I could take some pictures to show my family back home?"

"Of course you could, but you better ask permission."

"Should I ask permission from the Mount of Olives?" Click. Click. Simha smiled. "Which way to your kindergarten?"

"My kindergarten is not far from here, but I would like to take the longer road to show you our souks. I love them. Do you want to?"

"Yes. What's a souk?"

"A market. The Arabs call them souk, like in Hebrew *shuk*."

They crisscrossed Harat El Yahud Street in the Jewish Quarter. Locked behind iron gates and painted wooden doors, groups of low stone houses, crowded with families, surround communal courtyards, each containing its own water well. Towering above those dwellings, standing with thick arched stone walls and glistening domes, built over time, lying layer upon layer of past history are various synagogues: Ramban, Hurva, Tiferet Israel, Or Mitzion, Yohannan Ben Zakai.

Engraved in stone, above a blue painted door, is a Star of David with something written in its centre. Simha was busy counting the pinkish stones on the alley pavement.

"Simha, what's written inside this Star of David?"

"I don't know, I can't read yet, but my father once taught me how to write the word *shalom*. It looks similar."

"What does shalom mean?"

"Everyone knows! Shalom means 'peace,' like in Arabic *salaam*."

"Why are there so many synagogues here?"

"My abaa told me that every group of Jews who come from different countries pray differently, have different customs and need their own synagogue."

"Who are those people in black wearing those trimmed fur hats?"

"Those are Hasidic Jews. They spend all day at the yeshivas studing the Torah."

"Don't you like them?"

"My father told me they never work. They just study."

Click. Click. "Where now?"

"You didn't ask them permission. They might be angry."

"I took pictures from behind. Where now?"

"Down those stairs to Hacotel Hamaaravi."

"Hacotel Hamavi?"

"No! Ha-co-tel Ha-ma-a-ra-vi, the Western Wall. Some call it the Wailing Wall.

"Wailing?"

"My father says that this wall and the Jewish temple that was once above it, before it was destroyed long ago, was built by a king, I think his name was Herod. It's the only remainder of that temple. We call it Har Habayit."

"I think the Arabs call it Haram El Sharif. That's where they built their mosques?"

Soon, they faced a narrow alley. On their right was the glorious, high, white wall. To see its top edge, they leaned against a Magreb Quarter stone house to their left and stared in awe. The upper edge of the white Kotel softly kissed the blue sunny sky. Plants with pinkish flowers took hold in the cracks between the piled up stones. Olive tree roots clung to one of the upper stones, caressing its smooth face, sucking its marrow.

"Amazing! The old masons were undoubtedly masters of their craft."

"Mason? What's that?"

"A stone carver."

"Oh! Stone carver. My uncle is a stone carver."

"What kind of stone does he carve?"

"He carves tombstones. He's the best."

"How do you know he's the best?"

"I know! He carved a beautiful olive tree onto my grandfather's tombstone.

"Did you see it?"

"Yes. For my abaa, this wall is the holiest place in the whole world."

"Is it?"

"Every Friday he comes with his friends to pray here."

"Here? How could they pray here? The houses on the left are so close; it looks like a deserted dirty alley. Where do they sit?"

"They don't sit; they stand, crowded."

All of a sudden, they were pushed into a tiny alley door along the houses of the Magreb Quarter. A caravan of loaded donkeys sauntered past. They watched them disappear into another alley, swallowed into the souk's stomach, leaving their droppings along the way.

"You know, last Friday I came here with my abaa for the evening Maariv prayers."

"What? Girls pray, too?"

"Yes, but only in the women's section. My abaa wanted me to pray beside him in the men's section so my mother dressed me as a boy."

"Disguised as a boy?"

"I'd rather be a boy beside my abaa than a lonely girl with strange women in the women's section."

"What about your mother?"

"She doesn't like to come here. There are too many dirty animal droppings."

They continued walking towards the markets. Storeowners bent down to unlock the folding metal doors, pulling, then pushing them up, so they wrap like carpets around the iron poles above the entrance. People: Jews, Arabs, Christians of all ages, rushed through the narrow alleys in opposite directions. Some walked towards the markets and Shaar-Yafo, the Jaffa Gate, and some headed to churches in the Christian Quarter, or to mosques in the Muslim Quarter, or Jews to synagogues in the Jewish Quarter.

"My abaa forbids me to enter churches or mosques."
"Why?"
"He says it's a sin for Jews to be there."
"Why is it a sin?"
"My abaa says that Jews never ever worship icons. We are now in Souk el Dahab, the Gold Market. Do you want to see it?"
"Yes. Have you been here before?"
"Oh, yes. Recently my parents celebrated their anniversary. We came here to choose the golden necklace that my abaa bought my ima as a gift."
"Let me capture this dazzling alley." Click! Click!

The dozens of sparkling stores on both sides of the alley were lit with hanging kerosene lamps, displaying varieties of gold jewellery: rings, bracelets, necklaces, earrings and brooches. The glass showcases hanging on the walls were loaded with golden pendants of crosses, Stars of David and golden crescents. Ahmed stood in the entrance to his store, smiling.
"Sabach-el-cher, Simha! What are you doing here so early

in the morning?"

"Sabach-el-cher, Ahmed! I'm showing our guest your souks."

"What did he say, Simha?"

"He's greeting us with 'good morning.' "

"Simha, how come you speak Arabic?"

"My father's friends teach us Arabic and we teach them Hebrew like Suleman Abu Ibrahim. I love to play with Ibrahim."

"Who is Ibrahim?"

"Suleman's son.

"*Ta-alu*! Come in! Let me prepare Turkish coffee for you," offered Ahmed.

"Simha, how do we say thank you in Arabic?"

"*Shukran!*" the guest turned to Ahmed: "*Shukran!* We'll come for coffee some other time. Simha, let's go!"

On their way out, Simha said: "*Salaam Alekum!*"

Ahmed responded: "*Alekum Salaam,* Simha! Don't forget to send my blessings to your parents."

"What did he say?"

"*Alekum Salaam* means 'peace upon you,' like in Hebrew *Shalom Alechem*."

"Shalom! This reminds me of the word engraved in stone we saw earlier."

They reached the Silver Souk. On both sides of the alley, they saw abundant displays of silverware. Shelves from floor to ceiling were loaded with lustrous silver, candelabras, tea and coffee pots, plates, goblets, and cutlery. Glass showcases were crowded with silver jewellery engraved with geometric black patterns. On shelves behind the merchant were a large variety of freestanding crosses, Stars of David and silver crescents with stars in their centre. Watching the showcase beside the entrance door closely, Yusuf, the vendor, jumped out of his chair and rushed with a big smile.

The guest turned to Simha: "Perhaps I'll buy something for my mother. She loves silver jewellery."

"Sabach-el-Cher, Simha! How is your mother? She was sick last week?"

"Sabach-el-Cher, Yusuf! She is much better now."

"What does Sabach-el-Cher mean?"

"I already told you! Good morning!"

"It seems like you know everyone here, Simha."

"Last year, for my fifth birthday, my ima bought me this ring, bracelet and necklace here from Yusuf."

Yusuf interrupted: "Simha! Where is your necklace? Do you remember how long it took you to choose it?"

"I wear it only on Shabbat."

"Come in! Sit down!" Yusuf bowed. "The Turkish coffee is ready."

"Shukran Yusuf! We are in a rush, but tell me, are you a Muslim?" asked the guest.

"Of course I am. I pray five times a day. Why?"

"How come you're selling religious objects of other faiths?"

"You mean the Christian crosses and the Jewish Stars of David?"

"Yes."

"Well, let me tell you something!!! Our customers, whether they are Jews, Christians or Muslims, are our kings. No discrimination here."

"I like that. I'll be back."

"Your visit will be blessed."

They entered a ceramic store full of striking colours. A woman turned to the man beside her, whispering: "A feast for the eyes. What a feast." Elaborate ornamentations of reds, yellows, greens, blues and whites were dazzling. Shelves, tables and floors were overloaded with glazed vases, plates, goblets, cups, egg holders and spoons of every size imaginable. A woman, examining a pile of plates, began the long bargaining ritual.

She turned to the merchant: "How much for this plate?"

"This one is twelve *mil*. I will let you have it for a *grush*."

"Simha, how much is a grush?"

"A grush is ten mil."

"What could you buy with a grush?"

"A grush is a lot of money. You can buy a basket of eggs or three rotels of tomatoes or ten large cones of ice cream."

Agitated, the woman yelled at the merchant: "It's too much. I can get it for less at your neighbour's. Goodbye!"

As she walked to the door, the merchant called: "Hey! Lady, come back! I'll give it to you for nine." She didn't answer. "How much do you want to pay?"

She turned around: "Nine is too much."

"I'll give it to you for eight."

"What if I buy two?"

"What a beautiful woman you are! I will let you have two for seven mil each."

Ignoring his flirtation, she challenged him further: "What if I buy 12?"

With an attempt to hide his excitement at the prospect of such a big sale, he responded: "This is a different ball game. If you buy 12 you could have them for six mil each."

"Too much!" she said impatiently, on her way out the door.

The merchant ran after the woman: "Wait a minute, Lady! We just started. Why are you rushing?"

She turned around angrily: "I have no time. What is your last price? I don't see a line of people waiting to buy twelve plates in one shot."

"If you buy 12, you will pay five for each. This is my very best, last price!"

Determined, she responded: "I will take 12 and pay you two mil for each."

Pretending he was in shock, the merchant raised his shaking hands: "Are you joking? God is my witness! I swear on my mother's grave that I paid much more."

"Leave your mother out of this! I am not joking, only 24 mil for 12!" Sensing that the merchant was about to surrender, she stood firmly, raising her hands like a victorious warrior. "That's what I'm offering. Take it or leave it!"

Exhausted, desperate to sell, the merchant turned to her impatiently: "You know what, Lady? If you buy 12, you will pay only four groush. You can't get a better bargain."

Realizing that she could no longer push the price down, she said, as if doing him a big favour: "I will give you three groush for 12."

"Jesus! Allah-Rahim!" He raised his hands up in prayer.

"This is my last offer."

"Give me 3 and a half groush and they are all yours."

Stubbornly she said: "Only three groush. That's it."

Before totally surrendering, the merchant raised his head up to Allah begging: "Allah-ul-Akbar, help!" He tried his luck again by complimenting the woman: "You are a brilliant, tough bargainer, your husband Alli, I know him, should be very proud—saving him all that money."

Ignoring his compliments, she hovered at the door. "I have to go."

With desperation, he quietly said: "Your price is too low. I can't accept it."

Opening the door, she cried: "That's my last price. Three groush for 12!"

After a long pause, the merchant finally said: "Let me see! I can give you 12 for three groush only if you choose small plates."

"No!" she said sharply while her hands pointed animatedly: "I am going to choose four small of those, four medium of those and four large of those. That's what I need."

"I can't let you have the large plates for less than I paid."

"Pity. You leave me no choice but to buy them elsewhere."

She slammed the door behind her. The merchant ran to the door and called: "Wait Lady! Bargaining requires time and reflection."

"I have no time!"

The merchant, unwilling to give up, rushed towards her and prevented her from entering the next store. He then said softly: "Lady, Lady, listen to me, it is early in the morning—you're my first customer today—my lucky charm. Come in, start choosing your plates."

Watching this happen, the guest, wondering, turned to Simha.

"I can't believe this."

"Believe what?"

"That amazing lady. She bargained him down 80 percent of his asking price."

"My ima always says: 'Only the fools pay the full asking price in these markets.' If you don't bargain here, the vendors feel offended."

"Offended?"

FRUIT AND VEGETABLE VENDORS

"Denying them a game that everyone enjoys playing agitates them.

"Simha, who makes those ceramics?"

"The Armenians. They are the best."

"I would like to buy my sister one of those plates."

"Don't buy yet! My mother bought all our Passover dinnerware from the best Armenian craftsman. She will take you to his place in the Armenian Quarter, where you can find a larger variety, and cheaper, too."

They crossed the alley and entered a store of unglazed clay ware. Water jugs, called *jaras,* stood proudly on the shelves; their long spouts uniformly arranged like soldiers—their rifles all pointing in one direction. The floor was packed with large clay water containers, pots and bowls. Mounds of flat plates were stacked, one on top of another, crowding the aisles everywhere. Colours ranging from yellowish greys to reddish browns, peach and rusty oranges were spotted with black on account of their closeness to the oven fire. Excited, the guest looked through the camera lens. Click! Click!

"Who made those large pots?"

"Potters from Jericho."

"How do you know?"

"I saw them once when we went there to visit the hot springs. The potters in Jericho are wonderful. They make the pots on spinning wheels. I saw them. My abaa says that only unglazed jaras can cool water, if they are kept on roofs."

"On roofs?"

"The breeze up there keeps the water cool, even on hot summer days. Come on, let's go!"

"Wait, I don't want to miss this glass shop. Look at those endless shades of bubbled colours. Wow! Turquoise! Amber!

Emerald! White and opal! Click! Click! Who made those, Simha? I bet you know."

"Yes, I do. Glass blowers in Hebron."

"How do you know?"

"Last year, when we visited the tomb of Abraham in Hebron, my abaa entered the Machpela Cave to pray, and me and my ima visited the glassblowers. They made beautiful water glasses in front of our very own eyes, especially for my ima. She was so happy."

The guest, changing the film excitedly, took pictures one shelf at a time. Turquoise. Click! Click! Amber. Click! Click! Emerald. Click! Click! Opal. Click! Click!

They walked into one of the leather shops. A sharp smell of shoe polish invaded their nostrils. Hanging on the walls inside and outside the store were all kinds of leather coats in black, brown and beige. On the floor, between the tables, were piles of overflowing leather luggage. Displayed on rotating racks at the entrance were dozens of women's purses and school satchels. Simha examined one of the book bags.

"You like this one, Simha? Huh? Why don't we buy it for you, now?"

"Not now. My mother promised to buy me one when I go to *kita-alef*, first grade, but she has to order the right shoulder straps to keep my posture straight."

"Simha, look at that boy, carrying on his head a large aluminium plate loaded with strange-looking rounded bread, singing: *"Kaa-kaa! Kaa-kaa!* What does Kaa-kaa mean?"

"Kaa-kaa is the Arabic name for bagels."

"They smell so good! Let's have one. Hello, kaa-kaa boy! Come here! How much?"

"One mil each."

"Here are two mil for two."

The guest handed the boy two groush. Both Simha and the boy were shocked. Simha grabbed the coins, explaining that the guest was about to pay ten times more than needed. She handed the boy the two mil that her mother gave her that morning for drinks. Carefully, the boy removed the plate off his head, placed it on the sidewalk and wrapped two bagels in a newspaper for them. He then balanced the plate back onto his head and ran along, singing: "K-a-a-k-a-a!!! K-a-a-k-a-a!!!"

"Hey! Kaa-kaa boy!" yelled Simha, "come here! You forgot something!"
"What?"
"The *zaatar*."
"Here it is." He threw two small paper packages and continued his singing, "Kaa-kaa."
"What is *zaatar*?"
"It's a greenish powder of wild herbs, mixed with salt and sesame seeds. It's delicious when the kaa-kaa is dipped in. Here, try it!"
"Oh! It's delicious. De-li-cious!"

While strolling and enjoying their kaa-kaa, they reached a large, well-lit textile shop. Inside, were a huge variety of colourful fabrics wrapped in hundreds of cylindrical rolls: silk, cotton, crepe, organza, chiffon, satin, taffeta, and wool. Women examined the large tags that indicated the price per metre and the make: India, Italy, France, Spain, Damascus and England. Under the alley's rusty tin roof, men's *galabiya* gowns and heavily embroidered black women's dresses swayed softly in the morning wind. Taking more pictures, the guest urged Simha to move on. Simha refused, insisting on entering the store where her mother bought her wedding dress.

They entered. Dozens of drawers under the dark wooden counter were slightly opened and stuffed with endless laced patterns, all in different shades of white and in many sizes and shapes. Spread on the table were embroidered white tablecloths, sheets, napkins, and pillowcases. Hanging on the walls were long white muslin drapes, beautified with white needlework. Like a child in a toy store, the guest said over and again: "Amazing! A-ma-zing! I have never seen so many varieties of white. That wedding dress hanging above the entrance is stunning! Click! Click!"

Down the alley, they entered a carpet shop. Piles of layered rugs, each a different size, were spread on the floor. Leaning against the sidewalls were mounds of rolled up carpets, and hanging above them were small silk rugs with exquisite, shiny, velvety images of mosques, synagogues and churches. Portrayed on one of them was a young shepherd playing flute music to his sheep herd grazing on a mountain slope. On another, a young woman held a water jug on her head while dancing beside a water well.

"Simha, I like this beautiful dancing woman. Which one do you like?"

"This one."

"This old bearded man, the one bending over the balcony railing, talking to the crowd below? Why?"

"We have a similar one hanging at home. His name is Hertzel."

"Who is Hertzel?"

"My abaa told me that he's telling the crowd about his dream to establish a Jewish state to be named Eretz Israel"

"What's wrong with Palestine?"

"I don't know, but we need our own country. My father told me that Hertzel said: 'if you want it, it does not have to be a legend.' My father believes that one day the Hertzel dream will be realized and we will be safe in peace in our own land."

"Now I understand why Hertzel is so important. Let me take his picture." Click! Click! "A close-up one, too." Click!

They reached a large square with alleys radiating in all directions. At its centre, a solid old, deeply rooted olive tree with a large twisted trunk shaded most of the square. Scattered under its shade were tables and chairs occupied by men who drank coffee and played *shesh-besh*. A few wrinkled and bearded elders blew into fancy bottles full of bubbling water.

"What kind of pipes are those?"

"Suleman, my father's friend told me that those are water pipes for smoking tobacco. He calls them *nargila*."

"I have to take another picture!" Click! "Another one," Click! He took a deep breath, and looked around. "Simha, this labyrinth of alleys is so confusing. Which way should we take?"

"I don't know. I think we are lost."

"What street are we on?" the guest asked a passerby.

"Charat El Hadadin," said the man.

They found themselves in the middle of Charat El Hadadin, a street full of dark, long niches. Inside, ironsmiths beside their fire were busy, burning, welding, hammering and scratching all sorts of decorative railings for stairs, balconies, doors, window boxes and large gates.

Further down the alley, the bronze and brass casters were in the dark, humming and bustling molding, casting, scrubbing and shining all sorts of coffee tables, plates, bowls, pots and vases. The polished, shiny pieces were displayed outside on the alley stairs for everyone to see. They reached a dead end.

"Look, Simha! That alley is hardly wide enough for one person. Where does it lead?"

"I'm am not sure. I think that on the other side is the big *hamam*."

"Haman?"

"No, Ha – ma – m - m. My ima calls it the Turkish bath. Yesterday I was there with my parents for our weekly wash."

"Your mother and father bathe together in public?"

"Yes, but my abaa goes to the men's side; me and my *ima* to the women's side. I can't wait for next Thursday."

"Why Thursday?"

"My ima told me that as Fridays are devoted to cooking for the Shabbat, Thursday is our day for cleaning the house, laundry and our bath at the hamam."

"You really enjoy bathing in a crowded hamam?"

"Oh yes, very, very much!"

"Why?"

"To play with girls my own age in the most beautiful dreamy place. Yes, it's like walking into a world of marvel wrapped in marble. Everything in the hamam—walls, floors, sinks, taps, and benches—are made of white, pink and black marble flowers, birds and other beautiful shapes. I love painting them in my kindergarten."

"That sounds beautiful."

"Yes, but that's not all."

"What else?"

"In the centre of each hall, above the large, circular water basin, various marble animals spill hot water from their mouths, ears and noses."

"Really?"

"Yes, in cascades of, what my mother calls, 'singing, dancing water."

"She loves the hamam, too? Huh?"

"Oh, yes! Whenever we walk into the hamam, my ima stands, facing the waterfalls and prays: 'Bless you God, for this.' You know what my favourite is?"

"No."

"Do you want to know?"

"Yes!"

"The most beautiful of all is the view of the domed ceiling above the central hall."

"Why?"

"Well, inserted into the dome ceiling are blue glass tiles."

"You mean like mosaic?"

"I don't know what mosaic is. All I know is that the blue glass is so beautiful. At sunset, when the sun's rays come through the glass tiles, the steam and the haze inside rise up like blue soft caressing brushes. It is such fun to touch those foggy fingers! Such an exciting game to play!"

"To play? I thought you go to the hamam to take a bath?"

"Yes. After my ima finishes scrubbing my body, and cleansing it, she let's me wander around. Women of all ages undress in the dressing hall, walk into the washing halls, appear and disappear behind the heavy haze. Then they sit beside the hot waterfalls, scrub the dirt from their bodies with loofahs, wash their hair, rub their skin with aromatic soaps, and rinse with hot water collected in a shiny bronze *tasa*. You should see the delight on their faces. Some sing, others chat and then they walk into the steam hall under the blue glass dome, climb up onto the warm marble stage and rub their bodies with fragrant oils. My ima has a collection."

"Collection of what?"

"Fragrant oils." Simha counted the fragrances on her fingers. "Jasmine, rose, narcissus, rosemary, eucalyptus, orange and lemon. Every week my ima uses a different one. My abaa always uses the eucalyptus."

"What happens next?"

"After resting in the steam, then they walk back to the dressing room and just before putting on their freshly ironed clothes, they spray different kinds of perfume on their bodies."

"What kind of perfumes?"

"My ima has a collection of perfumes, too."

"Do you know the names?"

"I think so, one is amber, another is the coronation, the lavender, and I don't remember the rest. By the time we leave the hamam, we feel like new. It's a pleasure you should not miss!"

"I would love to."

"You would?"

They walked up the main alley. On their right, a large, blue ornamented iron gate stood ajar. They walked in. Inside, below the domed hall, vegetables were displayed in wooden stalls. Women chose the best vegetables and, while piling them up on one side of the scale, they argued price. The vendor balanced the scale with iron weights and jokingly wrapped up the price and their vegetables in old newspaper. Pyramids of shiny fresh vegetables attracted their eyes: tomatoes, cucumbers, peppers, eggplants, zucchinis and onions. Stacked high on the ground, in separate large mounds, were various watermelons: green, dotted white and yellow. Opposite them, a farmer sprayed water on his potatoes, beets and turnips. In another section, vendors sat behind fresh heaps of small, medium and large olives spread neatly on the ground. Beside them were rows of wooden barrels filled with pickled cucumbers, turnips, hot pepper, lemon and curry mango. Buckets overflowed with pickled black, green and purple olives. Along side, rusted tin pails were full of fresh bunches of green herbs: mint, coriander, basil, oregano, parsley, mirana and marjoram. In the corner, beside the shallots and garlic, were different types, colours and sizes of lettuce, cauliflower and cabbages.

Overhead, clinging to the suspended wooden poles, hundreds of pigeons performed their courting rituals. Some coupled, some kissed and caressed each other's necks, while others were frozen in a deep sleep. Above them, in the open windows of the central domed hall, chirping sparrows played joyfully, having a ball. Down below, wooden tables were jammed with fresh, dazzling colours of ripened late summer fruits: apricots, peaches, apples, pears and grapes. A merchant held up a cluster of large green juicy grapes and urged passers by to taste them, announcing loudly: "Anab El Chalil! Straight from El Chalil! Hebron! Hebron! The very best! The best!"

Facing him another vendor proudly displayed his early ruby red pomegranates and yellow quinces. He rubbed each of them delicately to bring out their natural shine and glow. Purple and green figs were piled in a heap beside the little, juicy, pinkish sycamore fruits. In separate stalls, leaning against the wall was the citrus section. It was filled with flaming oranges, lemons, clementines, grapefruits and pamelas. A seller holding a large pamela, the size of a watermelon, praised its beauty and heavenly taste with a song, declaring: "Straight from Jericho! Jericho! Jericho!"

He placed the pamela next to a mound of mini oranges, the size of grapes. Next, he picked up a cluster of oranges and praised their glorious taste and beauty with a different song, declaring "Straight from Nablus! Nablus! Nablus!"

In the dried-fruit section, women stood in line to be served by a busy vendor, surrounded with overflowing sacks of dates, figs, apricots, prunes, apples, raisins, pineapples and papayas. Neighbouring his stall, another merchant busy serving chattering women was surrounded by overflowing sacks of dry almonds cashew nuts, pine nuts—so many kinds of nuts. Beside him another vendor was surrounded by overflowing sacks of baked and unbaked seeds: sunflower seeds, melon seeds, watermelon seeds, sesame seeds, poppy seeds, cardamom seeds, coriander seeds, mustard seeds, pepper seeds - seeds of every imaginable type.

Two women, wearing black robes that were fully embroidered in red, sat on the ground resting their backs against the iron gate. In front of them were large baskets filled with *sabres* and *carob*. One woman turned to each and every passer-by: "Only one mil for ten sweet and juicy sabres. Here, try this peeled one!" The other woman urged the crowd: "Only one mil for a kilo of sweet carob. Here! Why don't you taste this?"

"Simha, what are those strange looking fruits?"

"Those are brown carobs. They are sweet and delicious to eat, but they are also used to produce a drink called *sus*. Those yellowish-red fruits are cactus fruits. We call them sabres."

All of a sudden he pulled Simha's hand and begged: "Please, Simha let's get out of here!"

"Why, what happened?"

"Look at my back! It's full of wet pigeon droppings!"

Outside in the alley, a man behind them screamed: "*Yaala! Yaala! Imshi!*"

"Why is he screaming?"

"He is asking us to move on, to clear the way."

Suddenly, they were shoved aside by a donkey's head and pushed into a tiny intoxicating spice niche whose owner was absent. An old man in a dirty gown was beating the donkey's ass with a wooden stick. Tightly strapped to the donkey's belly on both sides hung wooden boxes loaded with vegetables. On top of the donkey's back were two bamboo cages: one was crammed with brownish reddish hens and in the other were yellow chicks chirping madly. A folding table and chair and a large iron scale with heavy iron weights were tied to the roof of the cages. Dangling off the side of the cage was a brass coffee pot and a bunch of cups wrapped in cloth with a coffee-stained *primus*. On the other side, hung two large tin buckets filled with eggs. Atop this tower was a large bundle of hay, wrapped in a tattered blanket and attached to the top of all that were a few green glass bottles filled with liquid and a couple of red tin boxes.

"Unbelievable! How can one little donkey carry a weight larger and heavier than his own body?"

"My father says: 'Donkeys are born for hard work'"

"How on earth will this poor donkey get through this narrow alley?"

A tall, fat man pushed the donkey from behind, yelling and swearing that he was blocking the entrance to his spice store. Suddenly, he smiled. He recognized Simha and was glad to see her, claiming that he had something for her mother, asking her to get out of his store, but she couldn't. The donkey was blocking her way out. Mahamud pushed the donkey's ass and shouted: "Imshi! Move on!"

The agitated crowd waiting behind the donkey grew larger. Stubbornly, the donkey ignored the commotion and decided to take his break. Refusing to move, he splayed his hind legs, cementing them to the ground and, with great relief, he peed followed by an explosive fart and an enormous quantity of dung that splattered on the pavement. The donkey turned its head to assess the audience reaction. Curses and screams from the impatient crowd, who could hardly breathe, filled the air: "Imshi! Move on!!!

"Imshi! *Iben-el-kalb*! Move! Son of a dog!!!"

"Imshi! *Iben-el-sharmuta*! Move! Son of a bitch!!!"

"Imshi! *Ya-majnun*! Move! Deranged!!!"

Mahamud raised his head up to the heavens, begging: "Allah Rahim! God have pity on me!"

Looking down on the scene from up the alley, the bagel boy helplessly searched for a way down the steps. He watched the commotion, laughing hysterically.

"Idiot! What are you laughing about?" shouted Mahamud. "Why don't you help me pull this stupid donkey out of the way?"

The bagel boy, who stood on the higher steps looking down at the donkey, excitedly welcomed the challenge. He pulled the donkey's ears forward while Mahamud pushed the donkey from behind. The rebelling donkey bucked in disjointed movements, kicking Mahamud. Mahamud, who lost his balance, fell back onto the crowd behind. Everyone screamed and tumbled like dominoes, down the steps, their legs in contorted motion up in the air. The donkey ran amok, twisting in the air, knocking into the people and stalls on both sides of the alley. The large cowbell attached to his neck clanged madly. The first to fall was the bagel boy, his bagels

HASIDIC JEWS

strewn and squashed. The loaded boxes that were piled on the donkey's back came loose and tumbled down, crashing against the stony stairs. The hens and chicks escaped from their shattered cages and ran in all directions, seeking a place to hide. The buckets loaded with eggs, tumbled to the ground, smashing against the stone pavement, covering it with yellow and white slime. The donkey man looked up at the rusted tin roof, praised Allah for his glorious power and asked for mercy and forgiveness for all his sins.

Simha and her guest were finally able to leave the spice store so Mahamud could enter. He stuffed a brown paper bag full of small spice packages and tucked it into Simha's lunch box, asking her to give it to her mother. The fact the Simha didn't have the money, didn't bother Mahamud. Sending her away, he said: "Don't worry, Simha. Your mother never forgets to pay."

Simha and her guest continued to walk, climbing the alley stairs. Above their heads hung ropes of laundry, strung from balcony to balcony across both sides of the alley. Trousers, sheets, towels, underwear dripped onto the pedestrians below. A woman, whose balcony was full of red geranium pots, beat her carpets with a wooden stick, spraying the air with heavy clouds of dust that slowly descended on passersby.

A strong smell of meat and blood surged across from the gate on their right. Inside, facing the gate, were fish stalls. Various kinds of fish shimmered grey, black, silver and pink, all displayed in neat lines on a bed of ice chips with their eyes looking in the same direction. On the left side of this market, hanging on large iron hooks, skinned and split, were the remains of slaughtered lambs, sheep, goats and cows. Their heads dangled down, spilling blood on the floor. A man hosed the blood mixture towards the open sewer in the street. On a solid wood table, another man with a heavy iron axe split the meat and bones and threw each piece onto the appropriate mound: legs, shoulders, ribs, hearts, kidneys and so on. Millions of energetic humming flies, like hungry bees sucking a flower's nectar, had a feast, devouring the blood from the hanging, slaughtered animals' flesh. A woman interrupted the butcher: "Do you have a sheep's tail?"

"Yes," said the butcher, pulling a large sheep's tail from under the table. He handed it to the woman and she pushed it away.

"This is no good."

"Why? It's a good, large tail."

"No good, no good." She pushed it away and held her nose, mumbling. "This sheep had diarrhoea. Show me another one."

The butcher handed her a smaller sheep's tail from under the table. She examined it. "I'll take this one only if you peel off the skin and clean the wool. All I need is the fat."

They continued to bargain as the vendor peeled off the skin. Someone turned to the woman: "Do you use this fat for human consumption?"

"Of course. We love it, especially when it's deep-fried. It's a delicacy straight from the Garden of Eden."

The poultry section was abundant with butchered pigeons, turkeys, ducks, hens and cocks.

"What are those tiny creatures?" a European man asked.

"We call them *asfurs*," said the butcher.

"What does asfurs mean?"

"Asfurs are sparrows, like the ones up there."

"You eat them?"

"We do, and they are delicious."

With unimaginable speed and precision, a woman behind a neighbouring table plucked feathers from dead chickens, then passed them off to a man to hang on the line of hooks overhead. Meanwhile, under the stalls, a man squeezed live chickens into bamboo cages. A woman, who chose one of the chickens, refused to pay.

The angry butcher yelled: "Hey Lady! You have to pay before you take it away."

"I will pay only if I find the *Shohet*!"

"Go and find the Shohet, but leave the chicken here. In the meantime, Simha explained to her guest what Shohet means. She said: "My ima told me that Shohet is a Jewish man who is trained and authorized to slaughter animals according to the Jewish law. He ensures the meat Jewish people eat is kosher."

"Shohet! Shohet! Where are you?" cried the woman.

Suddenly Simha felt dizzy and nauseated. Her knees shook and she was about to faint. She rushed out of the meat market and sat on the alley pavement with her head between her knees. The guest ran after her.

"Simha? You look so pale."

"I am scared. Something terrible happened here last week."

"What happened?"

"Last week I was here with my ima. She was looking for the Shohet too. Suddenly we heard men's voices outside, screaming in Arabic: "*Edbach-el-Yahoud*!""

"What did they mean?"

"They meant 'slaughter the Jews!'" Then we heard a woman desperately screeching in Hebrew: '*Hatsilu*! *Ezraa*! Save me! Help!' We rushed outside and saw a woman lying on the ground beside that lemonade vendor. Her body was covered with stab wounds and her blood spilled everywhere. No one dared to help her. Everyone was too scared, except my ima."

"What did she do?"

"She begged all the donkey riders to take the woman to the hospital, but they all ran away. Finally, she gave one of them a lot of money and he agreed to carry the woman to the hospital. My ima went with him and left me all alone here."

"She left you alone? "

"My ima told me later that she did not trust the donkey rider to bring her to the hospital so she went with him to make sure. She said he might have dumped her somewhere and ran off with the money."

"Why would he do that?"

"My father told me that Arab people do those things."

"There were no police?"

"Even if there were, they would have helped the killers, not the woman. My father often complains about how the British authorities always appoint Arab policemen here."

"What happened to you?"

"All my ima managed to say was: 'Simha, run home immediately!' I did. Scared like hell. I ran so fast as never before. Only when I reached home did I feel safe, but I was worried about my ima."

"I would have been scared, too."

"My ima came back home late that night and said that the woman died in the hospital."

"Do you know why she was stabbed?"

"I really don't. Some Muslim people hate Jews. That's all I know. This was not the first stabbing. It happened many times before. I was told that a few years before I was born, Arab people ransacked Jewish homes in Hebron and killed dozens of them."

"Who told you this?"

"My abaa. He constantly warns us: 'always watch your

back! You never know what evil is behind.'"

"Now I understand why your mother made me promise not to let you out of my sight. We both need a drink! How about this lemon slush? What do you call it?"

"*Baraad.*"

They bought their *baraad* from a young Arab boy when they heard, off in the distance, the sound of bells and chanting men. They saw, coming from the Via Dolorosa alley on their way towards the Holy Sepulchre Church, a procession of Christian priests. They were in full regalia and waved sacred incense as they walked behind a young man who carried a large, wooden cross on his back. They let them pass and continued towards the Jaffa Gate.

At the Jaffa Gate Square, tables and chairs were scattered in the shadow beneath a large fig tree. Arab waiters with dirty aprons served the men a breakfast of kaa-kaa that they dipped into their mint tea. Hordes of bees sucked on the fallen ripe figs sprinkled on the ground. Groups of uniformed boys and girls rushed to school. Owners pulled their burdened donkeys towards the markets down below. Men rushed on overloaded bicycles to various destinations.

"What's that imposing citadel with its glorious stone-tower?"

"That is *Migdal David*—David's Tower. I have never been inside. I was told that the British police use it as a jail."

"What a waste!"

"A waste of what?"

"To me, using an architectural beauty as a jail is a waste. Simha! Look who is here! There, among the merchants, our donkey man is selling his goods."

They approached him. On his tattered blanket, the donkey

man sat beside his donkey that happily munched on his hay. The donkey man looked up at Simha while boiling his Turkish coffee in the *finjan* on his *primus* and said: "You look just like your mother."

"Do you know my mother?"

"Yes, of course. She buys my fresh eggs that I bring straight from my farm every week. Unfortunately, I have no eggs today."

They froze at the disturbing screech of a car behind the Jaffa Gate. A boy cried feebly: "Allah! *Daawoun*! God, help!" Everyone rushed towards the Jaffa Gate to see what happened. A boy laid face down on the ground, bleeding. The curious crowd swelled: "What happened? What happened?"

An Arab policeman, dressed in a dark navy blue British uniform explained in an authoritative voice: "This poor boy rushed towards his mother on the other side of the road when this dirty Jewish truck driver hit him and ran. I am going to kill the bastard!"

The donkey man, who by now stood with his donkey in the front row, yelled: "How do you know he's Jewish?"

The policeman, resolved in his answer replied: "All I know, trust me, is that only Jewish people would do this."

The boy's mother rushed to her son, crying: "Ali! Ali! Ibni! Ali! Ali! My son!"

Holding his dangling, crushed body close, she turned him over in despair and raised her head up towards heaven, crying: "Allah Rahim! God have pity on him!" Then she begged the people around: "Please! Call for help! We need to take him to the hospital!"

Simha and the guest recognized the injured boy as the bagel boy. His bagels were scattered all around. He was badly wounded. The donkey man came to the mother's rescue. He spread a blanket on the donkey's back for the boy's body and lifted him onto the makeshift stretcher. He then wrapped him for warmth, and together with the boy's mother, they headed off to the hospital.

Quietly, with fallen faces, the crowd dispersed. Some walked down to the Mamila market; some went back inside the walls. Simha and her guest crossed the empty alley that split the Armenian Quarter. Sounds of women chatting and laughing behind the courtyard walls filled the air. A man in front of them carried a gigantic shiny copper kettle with dangling, jingling bells on his back. Rhythmically two concave bronze plates shook in his right hand, while he announced and sang his *sus* song to the empty alley:

"Sus! La la la! Gling!
 Sus! La la la! Gling! Gling!
 Sus! La la la! Gling! Gling! Gling!"

To the guest, this man looked like a mobile orchestra. Simha explained that the *sus* is a sweet brown drink made of carob, the one they saw in the market earlier. They rushed behind the sus man to catch up with him. The sus man heard their steps behind. He stopped and turned around to face them, then started to dance. On his head was a *tarbouch* - a red Turkish hat with dangling black silk tassels. To Simha, the tassels reminded her of an agitated horse's tail and his swollen kettle reminded her of her pregnant mother. The kettle hung on his back, wrapped in a woven red wool rug, decorated with geometric yellow, blue and green patterns. It had a very long shiny copper spout that extended from the base of the kettle belly high over the sus man's head. The spout looked like a giraffe's neck in Simha's animal books.

Hanging off the rug were strands of colourful glass beads and tiny bells. The sus man wore knee-high red socks that were crammed into battered, black rubber tire sandals. Slotted into his leather belt were drinking glasses. In his left hand was a small, bronze water kettle he used for rinsing the glasses after each use.

"Two glasses of sus, please. How much?"
"Two mil for two."
"Here is a groush, keep the change!"
Both Simha and the sus man were stumped. Finally, the speechless sus man opened his mouth: "This is too much, too much."
"That's for your singing and dancing."
"Shukran! Shukran! Shukran!"

The sus man, bowing in gratitude for the guest's unexpected generosity, hung the rinsing kettle on his belt hook and pulled out one glass. He then stretched his arm out and bent forward, allowing the narrow spill of the brown sus to flow straight from the giraffe-like spout over his head, precisely into the centre of the glass. Ceremoniously, he then straightened his back, allowing the foam in the glass to subside, and handed Simha a full glass of fresh brown cold sus. He repeated his trick for the second glass. While watching them drink, he danced and sang in his over curled voice to celebrate this special occasion.

The guest wanted to take a picture of the sus man, whom he thought was an amazing musician and acrobat. No one back home would ever believe that he could pour the sus from such a distance without spilling a drop. He remembered to ask the sus man's permission.

"Of course! Here, I'm ready. Go ahead."

With a smile of satisfaction all over his face, the guest clicked his camera again and again. From different angles again and again. Bowing, the guest said: "Shukran! Shukran! Shukran!"

"Shukran! *Ya habibi,*" said the sus man.

Simha volunteered the meaning of *Ya habibi:* "It means," she said, "my dearest."

Simha and her guest finally entered Harrat el Yahud in the Jewish Quarter. Sounds of singing boys were heard from behind the barred windows.

"Simha, is this your kindergarten?"

"No, this is the *Cheder* School, just for boys, like the *Kutab* that we saw in the Muslim Quarter earlier."

"Simha," he said, "could you please explain to me?"

"What?"

"Are there differences between Cheder and Kutab?"

"Yes. Cheder . . . is where the rabbi teaches the Jewish boys the Torah. Kutab . . . is where the Muslim *Imam* teach the boys the Koran."

"What about the girls?"

"Girls go to Gan-Ha-Yeladim Kindergarten. Here it is, on the second floor." Here is Sarah, my teacher."

"Simha, where have you been? We were very worried. It's almost lunchtime."

"I was showing our guest the souks..."

* * *

Simha wakes up. She had lost track of time and space. Her escape to faded childhood memories and her foggy mixture of dreams, visions and fantasies, does not make her frustration easier. With her coffee and the morning *Gazette* in hand, she sits beside the fireplace wondering why her home in Jerusalem never had a fireplace like her home in Montreal. Unlike Israel, where The Peace is placed on an unreachable, invisible pedestal, in Canada every single cell in the air smells of Peace. In Canada, land and water from sea to sea, are conquered and owned by Peace. In Canada, all creatures breath Peace, touch Peace, hear Peace, taste Peace. Peace is free for the taking—free for all.

Headlines this morning read the same as the days, weeks and months before. Again the endless cycle of violence between Israelis and Palestinians continue with no sign of relief. When will we be freed from our encaged rage, imprisoned in our past?

THE *SOUS* VENDOR

ARCHES IN THE OLD CITY

Burial on The Mount of Olives:
excerpt from an unpublished novel: Olive Trees

When Malka was about five years old, her grandfather, Mored-Chai, passed away. Malka loved him. She used to call him *Sabaa*. She remembers how she sat on his lap, tied to his chest by his strong arms, listening to stories of how God created the world in six days and kept the Shabbat just for rest. Often he would cuddle her and whisper into her ear: "My little child, my beauty, you are going to be Malka, a queen."

"Sabaa, how do you know?"

"I know my child, I know. We didn't name you Malka for nothing."

"What do you mean, Sabaa?"

"You were born on the day of Purim. On that day we celebrate Queen Esther's victory over Haman, our enemy, who wanted to destroy our people."

"Sabaa, who is Haman?"

"Haman was the highest ranking advisor to King Ahashverosh, who lived many years ago and reigned over the 127 provinces stretching from Hodu to Kush."

"Where is Hodu and Kush?"

"Hodu is India and Kush is Ethiopia. A vast, vast kingdom it was."

"Why did Haman want to kill the Jews?"

"Hatred, my child, blind hatred. In his outrage, Haman the evil issued a decree to destroy all the Jews just because Mordechai the Jew, who was Esther's uncle, didn't bow to him. Jews never bow down to or worship other people, ever. They bow only when praying to God. Remind me to tell you the story about Hannah and her seven children, who were killed by King Antiyochus just because they refused to bow to him."

"Anti...Anti...what?

"An-ti-yo-chus. The king who destroyed our temple."

"Who is Esther?"

"Remember the story I told you last Purim?"

"No."

"Well, Esther was an orphan."

"Sabaa, what is orphan?"

"Orphan is a child whose parents are dead."

"Why did her parents die?"

"I don't know. The Bible doesn't tell."

"What happened?"

"To whom, Esther or Haman?"

"To Esther."

"Well, legend has it that her uncle, Mordechai, raised her to be wise and beautiful. King Ahashverosh was searching for a new wife to replace his first one, Vashti, who disobeyed him. He sent commissioners throughout his provinces with an order to bring all the beautiful virgins for him to choose from."

"What is a virgin?"

"An unmarried woman."

"What happened to Esther?

"She came, among hundreds of them, and the king chose her as his queen, but she didn't tell him that she was Jewish."

"Why? You told me that we Jews should be proud."

"Mordechai told her not to tell."

"Why not? Wasn't she proud?"

"She was proud, but because Jews were hated then, they had to cover up their identity."

"How do you know?"

"I just told you. Haman issued a decree to annihilate the Jews."

"Annihilate?"

"To kill them—to make them vanish from the face of the earth. Only after Esther became the queen did she then tell the king her secret."

"What secret?"

"The secret that she was Jewish."

"Did he kill her for lying?"

"No. The king loved Esther very much, so he cancelled Haman's decree then gave Esther and Mordechai the power to take care of the Jews and the Jews were saved."

"How do you know?"

"Here is the proof. Listen, it is inside this *megilat Esther*, part of the Bible: *The King Ahashverosh said to Queen Esther and to Mordechai the Jew, You may write concerning the Jews whatever is favourable in your eyes, in the name of the king, and seal it with the king's signet, for an edict may not be revoked.' Then the city of Shushan was cheerful and glad.* Since then, every 13th day of the month of *Adar*, we celebrate Purim."

"That's why you named me Malka?"

"Yes, that was the first reason. The second is that you are very special."

"Am I?"

"Yes. You are the first, born to your mother Ruth, and she is my first, born like me, the first, born to my father. You are my first grandchild, too. You are going to have many brothers and sisters and as the firstborn you will take care of them, like Queen Esther took care of our people."

In those days, when Mored-Chai bent his head to kiss Malka's neck, his long, grey beard tickled her and she would pull away. Before she ran off, he always slid his hand deep into his pocket, pulled out a candy and gave it to her with his blessing: "Have a sweet day, Malka."

The first pencil she was ever given was given to her by Mored-Chai.

"With this," he said, "you are going to learn how to write the Hebrew alphabet." He handed her a shiny blue pencil.

"Sabaa," Malka said, "I can't write with an unsharpened pencil."

"I know. Here is one mil. Go to the alley on the right and you will find, beside the *Madrassa* – you know where the Madrassa is?"

"Yes, where the Muslim boys sing the Koran."

"Beside the Madrassa entrance you will find a man with a new invention—a little shiny machine with a hole and a rotating handle attached to a wooden tripod. They call it a pencil sharpener."

"A machine that sharpens pencils?"

"Yes, all you need to do is push the pencil into the hole, turn the handle a few times and a miracle! The pencil is sharpened perfectly."

"I would like to try that."

"Don't try, it's dangerous. Just give him this *mil* and he will sharpen your pencil. Come back immediately. I'll wait for you."

Malka faithfully obeyed her grandfather. She found the man next to the Madrassa with the pencil sharpener, stood in line behind the other children and waited her turn.

With her sharpened pencil in hand, she sat on her grandfather's lap and, on a piece of paper, he wrote, saying out loud: "This... is... *aleph*, the first letter in the Hebrew alphabet. Copy it. Here. Carefully." She did.

Glancing at her, he said: "This is nice, Malka, but your aleph is limping."

"Limping?"

"Yes. One of your aleph's legs is much longer than the other. Imagine yourself with one leg longer than the other. You would limp, right?"

"Right."

"Try again, my sweetie." She did. Caressing her hair, he examined her second aleph, and said softly with a smile: "This aleph is very sick."

"Why sick?"

"Look at its two heads. One of them is all right, but the second one is falling like a sick, sad man. The aleph's head should be stretched up, healthy and proud."

"Why proud?"

"Aleph the first of our letters, the leading one. It has to be proud."

In those days Mored-Chai tried to make Malka laugh on many occasions. For each and every letter of the alphabet, he pulled a funny story from his sleeve, like a magician.

"How come the aleph is the leader?"

"Let me tell you a story."

"About what?"

"About how in time immemorial, the aleph was chosen to be the first. Long, long ago all the letters assembled to choose their leader—the first letter of the alphabet. The debate lasted all night with no conclusion. At dawn, the letter *shin* declared that it should be the first. 'Why?' everybody raved. The *shin* said: 'I have three heads. I am the wisest. I should be the first.'

The letter *lamed* interrupted: 'I am the tallest. You can see me from big distances. I should be the front runner.'

'Look who is talking,' said the *yod*. 'Although I am the smallest, I deserve to be the first.'

'Is that so?' said the *rish*. 'And why is that?'

'I am very important. I appear in the name of God.'

'Me, too,' said the *hey*. 'Me, too.'

'So what?' said the *beth*. 'I deserve to be the first because, the book of Genesis begins with me, but in my opinion the aleph deserves to be the leader.'

'Why?' yelled the others.

'With two heads and two solid legs the aleph is exactly what we need.'

'No way,' said the letter *hey*, 'I have to be the first.'

'You can't!' said the letter *chet*. 'Your amputated leg, hanging in the air, makes you limp. I am for the letter aleph, too.'

'Why not me?' said the *samech*. 'The words, *sefer* or *sefarim*, meaning a book or books, could not exist without me. Imagine a world without books?'

'Yes, yes, the *samech* is right,' said the aleph. 'A world without *sefarim* has no meaning at all. Imagine our life without the Bible?'

'You are a closed circle, like a prison. No one can get in or out. You can't be our leader. We need someone with an open head, like the aleph,' said the letter *daled*.

'I am for the letter aleph,' interrupted the letter *beth* again. 'If you do not agree with me, let's have an election and the one who gets the majority of votes will be chosen as our leader.'"

All of a sudden Mored-Chai became silent. Malka, curious, asked: "Sabaa, did you fall asleep? What happened?"

"About what?"

"About the election? How did it end?"

"Oh, yes. Well, the majority voted for aleph. Since then, aleph is the first letter in our alphabet."

That night at home, Malka eagerly copied the aleph many

times. Some were big or long, some small or short, some skinny, others fat. The next day, her grandfather was pleased: "This is beautiful, my child. I knew you were a fast learner, but we have to put everything in order."

"What do you mean?"

"I have a present for you."

"Another present?"

"Yes. A copybook. See, it has double lines to guide you where to start and where to end each letter. We are going to devote each page to one letter in the alphabet. Sit down, Malka. Today, I'm going to teach you the letter *beth*. If you're good, I will teach you the letter *gime,l* too."

A few weeks and many pencils later, Malka not only knew the alphabet by heart, but her copybook was full. Her grandfather was very proud, showing it to all his customers in the market: "Look at what my granddaughter Malka did. Isn't it beautiful?" he asked, hunting for compliments.

What bothered Mored-Chai was the cost of the pencils and the sharpening. It was costing him a bundle. One day, hand in hand with Malka, he rushed to see Naim.

"Who is Naim?" Malka asked.

"The pencil sharpener," he grumbled.

"*Qif-halak*, how are you, Naim?" asked Mored-Chai, approaching the pencil sharpener.

"Thank God, I am healthy," said Naim. "and how are you Mored-Chai?"

Mored-Chai went straight to the point: "I paid you 35 mil to sharpen my granddaughter's pencils for the last four weeks. This is too much; it doesn't even include the cost of all the pencils I had to buy."

"How much do you want to pay?" asked Naim in a comforting voice.

"I'll pay you one mil per week. That's it. If you don't agree,

I will sharpen her pencils with my razor. Here is four mil in advance for the next month. What do you say?"

"God bless you Mored-Chai, of course I agree," said Naim, who preferred to get four mil per month instead of nothing. They shook hands.

From that day on, Naim sharpened Malka's shrinking pencil stubs. After the first month, instead of four mil, Mored-Chai brought Naim a big jar of pickled olives to express his gratitude. For Naim, it was a better deal because the olive jar was worth ten mil; his payment more than doubled.

One summer day, Mored-Chai was sitting in the shade of the olive tree in his courtyard peeling an orange and sharing its juicy flesh with Malka.

"I planted this olive tree before you were born." Raising his head, glancing up at the olive tree branches, he added: "This tree was very small—smaller than you are now. Look how widespread its branches are, like an umbrella, and see how beautiful its silvery leaves are."

"Sabaa, why did you plant an olive tree?"

"Of all the fruit trees on God's earth that I love dearly: dates, oranges, pomegranates, figs, carobs, almonds and grapes, my favourite is the olive tree."

"Why?"

"The olive tree is part of our people's history. It has many meanings."

"Like what?"

"The olive tree means plenitude, peace between people, hope, and protection from the sun, wind and rain," he said pointing at the shade all around them.

"But other trees provide shade, too."

"Yes, but the olive tree gives us fruit."

"Other trees give us fruit."

"The olives allow us to produce olive oil. Remember what we did last Hanukah with the olive oil? We lit our *Hanukiya* for eight nights."

"Why do we do that?"

"To remember the miracle."

"What miracle?"

"When the Makabis took over our temple that was destroyed by the Romans, they found a jar with enough olive oil to light the flame for one night, but miraculously it lasted eight nights."

From his pocket, always full of goodies, Mored-Chai pulled out a small wooden snuffbox. "Look at this Malka. This was carved from olive tree wood. Isn't it beautiful?" He took a pinch of tobacco, sniffed it, sneezed with great satisfaction, and added: "You know Malka, in our Bible there are plenty of stories about olive trees. Do you want to hear one?"

"Yes."

"Hand me the Bible. Here is the first Biblical story where the olive tree is mentioned. *Noah was a righteous man, perfect in his generations; Noah walked with God. Noah had begotten three sons: Shem, Ham and Japheth.* You know, we are the descendants of Shem…"

"Who are the descendants of Ham?"

"The blacks in Africa are the descendants of Ham."

That was the first time Malka ever heard the name Africa.

"Are you listening, Malka?"

"Yes."

"Let's continue. *Now the earth had become corrupt before God; filled with robbery. God said to Noah: 'The end of all flesh has come before Me. Make for yourself an Ark of gopher wood; make the Ark with compartments, and cover it inside and out with pitch.'*"

"Sabaa, I thought you are going to tell me a story about an olive tree."

"Patience, my child. Reading the Bible needs patience. Listen to what God said to Noah: *I am about to bring the Flood-waters upon the earth to destroy all flesh in which there is a breath of life from under the heavens; everything that is in the earth shall expire. But I will establish My covenant with you, and you shall enter the Ark—you and your sons, your wife, and your sons' wives with you. And from all that lives, of all flesh, two of each shall you bring into the Ark to keep alive with you.*"

"Why two of each?"

"Because only a couple, one male and one female can produce new life."

"Why an ark?"

"To save them from drowning in the flood—let me continue?"

"*In the six hundredth year of Noah's life...*"

"Sabaa, 600 years! How old are you?"

"I am 60."

"Are you old?"

"Yes."

"How much is 600 years?"

"It's ten times longer than my whole life."

"Are you going to live as long as Noah?"

"I don't think so."

"Why?"

"Nowadays, one rarely could reach the age of 100."

"How was Noah able to live 600 years?"

"That's what the Bible says. People lived longer in those days."

"What happened to Noah?"

"Here it says: *All the fountains of the great deep burst*

forth; and the windows of the heavens were opened. And the rain was upon the earth for forty days and forty nights. And it came to pass at the end of forty days, that Noah opened the window of the Ark and then he sent out the dove from him to see whether the waters had subsided from the face of the ground. But the dove could not find a resting place, and it returned, for water was upon the surface of the earth. He waited again another seven days and then sent out another dove from the Ark. The dove came back to him in the evening—and behold! An olive leaf! It had plucked with its bill! And Noah knew that the waters had subsided from upon the earth."

"So, what happened to the olive tree?"

"The olive tree grew, gave fruit and came to signify peace on earth.

"Sabaa, why were you named Mored-Chai instead of Mordechai like everyone else?"

"You mean like Queen Esther's uncle Mordechai, in the Bible?"

"Yes."

"Wise question, my beauty—very clever. Well, my name derives from Mordechai, but my mother Deborah, your great-grandmother—bless her soul—twisted the name to suit her feeling. She told me that when I was in her womb, I was kicking as hard as a rebel, so she named me Mored-Chai meaning 'Rebel Live On.'"

"How come I never saw Deborah?"

"Deborah died in Baghdad before we came to Jerusalem, where you were born. Do you know after whom she was named?"

"No."

"Well, during Biblical times, long, long ago, Deborah was a heroine. She was also a prophet, a judge and a great poet.

A TORAH READER

Should I read you her poem? *When vengeances are inflicted upon Israel and the people dedicates itself [to God]."*

"Sabaa, please, not now."

During that time, Mored-Chai convinced his rabbi to accept Malka as a pupil in his cheder. Malka hated that cheder. She was the only girl among the boys and often ran away to find her grandfather at the market where he sold his pickled olives. It was not easy to find him. Every day he sat in a different souk alley. Why? "To attract new customers," he explained.

No one knew his real name. They called him The Pickle Man Prophet. He sat on the ground leaning against the wall, wrapped in his large, white wool gown with his knees bent close to his chest. His body looked like a square box, his grey hair swept back full and majestic, like a lion's mane. His rippling beard descended down his chest. Jars, of all different sizes, were full of pickled olives on the ground beside him. He preached lessons of morality to any passerby, whether they were Jews, Christians or Muslims. To prove his point, he quoted straight from the Bible.

On one of Malka's visits, he was bargaining with Ali, an olive grower from the village of Lifta. Mored-Chai knew Ali for many years. Every summer, he bought olives from him and they became friends. Last year Mored-Chai even went to Lifta for Ali's young daughter's wedding. On that day, in the market, he bought two sacks of fresh green and purple olives from Ali but he complained: "Ali, your olives are not only the most expensive, but every year you charge more. Why? Does God charge you more for the rain?"

"The rain is God's blessing; my olives are expensive because they are the best. It took me years of hard work to reach that quality. If you want cheaper olives, buy them from the olive growers in Hebron or Bethlehem."

"But they are not as juicy as yours."

"There is your answer," Ali responded. Before he left Ali added: "Send my blessing to your wife, and tell her that soon I'm going to have my first grandchild. I hope that both of you will be there for the celebration."

Mored-Chai paid a donkey owner to load and deliver the olives to his home. Hand in hand with Malka, they walked in front of the donkey to show the way. It was a scorching hot summer day. While crossing the Armenian Quarter, Mored-Chai stopped beside a sus vendor and bought a glass of the fresh sus for the three of them.

The next few days Mored-Chai didn't go to the souk. He was busy pickling the fresh olives. Simha, his wife and Malka's grandmother, unhappy like always, complained: "If you don't go to the market, you will loose your clientele."

"Don't worry, Simha," he said. "They will end up buying from me anyway because my pickled olives are the best."

In the next few afternoons, after the cheder class, Malka joined Simha. They sat on small wooden stools under the olive tree and, with a small river stone, beat the olives, hammering each against a large, flat rock then throwing the crushed ones into a large bowl. Mored-Chai gathered up the beaten olives in his large wrinkled hands and threw them into a tall clay jar, pressing, compressing and squishing them down, then pouring on a layer of salt. He squeezed another layer of beaten olives and more salt until the jar was full to the brim. He covered it with a matching clay lid, wrapped the top of the jar with a cloth and wound a piece of rope to seal it tightly. Stretching his back, taking a deep breath with a content smile he said: "*Bezrat hashem*, with God's help, in a few weeks, those olives will be ready for sale." Simha, with undying hope nagged: "Mored-Chai, when are you going to buy me a loom? I want to start with my weaving."

"With God's blessing, next year."

"That's what you've been saying for the past five years. Next year, next year, next year. How long should I wait?"

The day Malka went with her parents to synagogue, all dressed in black, was a winter day she will never forget. A line of black carriages with agitated horses stood like chariots beside the synagogue entrance. The nervous horses were waving their tales to ward off the cloud of flies on their backs. Anxious, in the pouring rain, they scratched their metal horseshoes in the puddles against the stony pavement. The sound of rolling thunder agitated them further. They swayed their heads so that the bells hanging around their necks jingled loudly. Soaking wet, people from all directions rushed towards the synagogue.

"Abaa, why is the synagogue so full of people today?"

"They have all come to pay their last respects to Sabaa Mored-Chai."

At the end of that long boring ceremony, the wooden coffin wrapped in Sabaa's *Talit*, his white prayer shawl, was carried out and placed on the front seat of the first carriage. A few shovels were tied to the back of the carriage. On the seat behind the coffin, Savta Simha, Malka's grandmother, squeezed between Ruth who was holding the baby and Moshe who held Malka on his lap. "Malka, please hold this package so I can hold on to you."

"What is it? It is so wet."

"It's a baby olive tree."

"Why do we need a baby olive tree?"

"You will see later."

When all the mourners took their seats in the carriages behind, Moshe ordered the Arab horsemen: "*Yala Imshi*! Move on." Passing through the Jewish Quarter alleys, the carriage convoy first stopped in front of Rabbi Yohannan

Ben Zakai Synagogue to allow Mored-Chai to say farwell to his congregation, then they exited the Old City wall through the Dunge Gate. The gallant horses gaily galloped; clip clopping at high speed down to the Kidron Valley. Malka was shaking with fear. Her father held her tight and said: "Don't be frightened, Malka. Everything is okay." To distract her from the fast sliding carriages, he said: "On our way back, I'm going to show you the lions."

"Real lions?"

"No, the four lions carved in stone above the Lions' Gate."

Simha jumped in. "Why through the Lions' Gate and the Muslim Quarter? It will make our route much longer and dangerous, too."

"We have to," said Moshe. "I have to return all the shovels to Suleyman. You know he lives in the Muslim Quarter. He needs them for tomorrow morning to dig the grave for his neighbour, who died from typhus last night."

Beside the gate of the Mount of Olives Cemetery, the carriages stood in line again. Moshe, with Shimon and Reuven, Malka's uncles, lowered the casket from the carriage and, with help of a few more men, they climbed up between the gravestones, in a slow procession, while the other mourners followed behind, reciting prayers and humming melancholic melodies. In the meantime, the rain stopped and the clouds took their leave, allowing the warm sunrays to comfort the mourners.

On the mountaintop, around the open grave, the mourners stood in two circles – one inside the other. In the inner circle, opposite Simha and her family stood Shira, Malka's aunt and her family, totally ignored. In the outside circle, the rest of the mourners stood. Among them, Malka recognized Suleyman, Zahra, his wife and Ibrahim, their son, who Malka was very fond of. Malka did not understand why

many were crying and some were beating on their chests
while spelling Mored-Chai's name. After the eulogies and
prayers, the coffin was lowered into the open grave and
people with shovels threw soil onto the coffin. Moshe
approached the fresh grave, lowered his head and, as if
talking to someone, he whispered: "Mored-Chai, you were
like a father to me. A father I never knew. You are here at
your last resting place, exactly where you chose to be. Bless
your soul."

At the end of the burial ceremony, the mourners, including
angry Shira and her family, returned to the waiting carriages,
leaving Simha with her family at the graveside. Moshe,
unable to hide his anger said to Simha: "This is unfair,
unforgivable."

"What?"

"How could you ignore Shira? She is your daughter, your
flesh and blood."

"She sinned," said Simha. "I will never make peace with
her. Don't mention her name ever again."

With revived energy, Moshe took a shovel, dug a hole
beside the fresh grave, and planted the young olive tree that
Malka had been holding. Gazing at Simha, expecting her
approval, Moshe said in a conciliatory voice: "Mored-Chai,
bless his memory, loved olive trees. Remember, Simha? It was
the first thing he did when you moved to your new home in
the Jewish Quarter."

"Yes," said Simha with a shade of anger, "Of course I
remember that olive tree. It grew so large I was not able to
plant vegetables anymore."

"You know, Simha," Moshe said, "he will be very pleased
that his grave will be shaded by an olive tree."

"Moshe?" asked Simha, sobbing. "Would you plant one
for me, too?"

"Of course," said Moshe, "Just tell me where."

"Here, beside my husband," Simha pointed. She stood for a while sobbing uncontrollably, then said: "It's time to go home."

After that day, once every week especially in the hot summer, Moshe, often with Malka, picked up buckets of water and climbed the Mount of Olives to water Sabaa's olive tree. This pleased Simha. Once she said to him, "You were like a son to Mored-Chai. Better than his own sons. They don't care about his grave."

Once a year, days before the anniversary of Mored-Chai's death, Simha ordered a few carriages to come and pick up the whole family, with at least ten men for the *Minyan* prayers. They travelled to the Mount of Olives, climbed to Mored-Chai's grave and read the *Kaddish*: "*Yitgadal Ve-yitkadash Sh'mey Rabbo. Be-ol'mo ...*

* * *

Now, years later, though Malka is a grandmother, she still longs for the strength of her grandfather's arms and the warmth of his lap. If only she could see him one more time, talk to him, touch him and play with the soft ripples of his beard . . . just once.

Here he is . . . in the middle of a severe ice storm . . . in her home . . . in Montreal, sitting on a colourful Persian carpet, wrapped in his large white wool gown. With his knees bent to his chest, his body still looks like a square box. His grey hair sweeps back full and majestic, like a lion's mane, his rippling beard descends down his chest as he faces the roaring firelight. The wrinkles on his face seem to be ploughed deeper than before. His hair, once grey, is now radiant snow white, glowing like a halo of golden light. His once-long beard now is much longer, resting softly on the Persian carpet. His strong muscular arms, now feeble, trembling, skin and bone. His eyes are shrunken, sunken deep. His toothless wide-open mouth is like a twisted trembling question mark. She could not imagine sitting on this man's lap anymore. On the contrary, it would be more appropriate for her to hold him on her lap. Still, his wondering, wise eyes glance at her, thoughtfully asking: "Who are you?"

"Your granddaughter."

"Which one. I had many."

"Your first."

"I had a first grandchild with each of my children. What's your name."

"Malka."

"Oh! Malka, Malka, of course I remember. You were my favourite. You're so different now."

"I'm a grandmother now."

"I remember you as a little child. Why are you in Canada and not in Israel, where you were born and belong?"

"It's a long story."

"Aren't you ashamed?"

"Ashamed of what?"

"Ashamed of abandoning your family, betraying your country and turning your back on your people. Shame! Shame! I was elated up there in heaven when in 1948, finally, after 2,000 years of wandering, the land of Israel finally became ours. And you left? Just like that? Left? You'd better explain."

"Sabaa, some other time."

"Now! Now! I need your explanation now!"

"Well...yes. We are free now, in our own land, but there is no peace, no peace at all. Innocent people and children are killed everyday."

"So, that's why you called me?"

"Yes, a few questions have haunted me since childhood."

"Answers? You want answers now? After all these years?"

"Yes."

"Dear Malka, when you were a child, I used to share my mint tea with you. We drank it from the same glass, remember?"

"Yes, I remember you liked your tea very hot. It burned my tongue."

"Yes, my dear. For every good thing in life, there is a price to pay, but I cooled the tea for you. Don't you remember?"

"I do."

"The tea we drank together was a combination of four principles that guided me all my life."

"I don't understand?"

"Well, consider the essential; if all human beings on the face of this earth are equal and want to live in peace—the peace described in our Torah—then they need to respect each other, to share their life experiences, understand and compromise. I applied these principles with all my friends, no matter who they were: Christian, Muslim or Jew."

"All I remember from my childhood is that you were friendly with everyone and they all loved you."

"Exactly, like our Torah says: *Love your neighbour as much as you love yourself.* Please, Malka, could you make me a glass of mint tea?"

"Of course. I have some already made. Here it is."

"Thank you, Malka! Oh God, this tea is from heaven. So, what do you want to know?"

"Why Sabaa, is the peace that everyone yearns for out of our reach?

"Well, the peace question that we and other nations

struggled with for centuries was actually unachievable because, well, you answered it yourself."

"Me?"

"Yes. You said that innocent people and children are killed everyday. Right? This would not happen between people who respect and understand each other. Many mistakes were made by politicians on both sides, like the settlements."

"This is true, Sabaa, but we could not change the past. Where do we turn now?"

"Elect leaders on both sides with high moral standards."

"Sabaa, it sounds like utopia."

THE RABBI YOHANAN BEN ZAKKAI SYNAGOGUE

THE WEST SIDE OF MOUNT OLIVES CEMETERY

Tombstones

The euphoria during and after the Six Day War, which started on June 5th, 1967, grabbed the population of Israel into a mighty vortex. Radios all over the country were open non-stop day and night, crowding the air with astonishing, rushing, sublime news. Headlines in the daily newspapers, which often printed second and third editions, overwhelmingly circulated the exciting news and images.

* *In Few Hours the Israeli Airforce Destroyed Most of the Egyptian, Jordanian and Syrian Air Forces.*
* *The Sinai Peninsula is in our hands.*
* *The Egyptian Army is in Retreat.*
* *Ariel Sharon, Battalion, Crossed the Suez Canal.*
* *The Road to Cairo is Wide Open.*
* *The Golan Heights Under IDF Control.*
* *The Syrian Army in Retreat.*
* *The Road to Damascus is Wide Open.*

Ecstatic disbelief screamed from every smiling face. What really occupied the Israeli mind was East Jerusalem: the Old City, the Jewish Quarter, Mount Zion and the City of David, the Mount of Olives, and above all, the Kotel and the Temple Mount. People were glued to the radio, waiting. The news came on June 7th, 1967, in a chain of startling, crowded reports that continued to vibrate the air at high speed.

* *The Mount of Olives Controlled by the Jordanian Army is Ours Again.*
* *The Old City of Jerusalem Liberated by the Special Unit of IDF Paratroopers.*
* *Israeli Soldiers are Praying at The Kotel Once Again.*
* *The Synagogues in The Jewish Quarter, Turned to Rubble by the Jordanians, Will be Rebuilt.*

Mota Gur's thundering voice over the radio declared on June 7th : *Temple Mount is in our hands. Repeat. Temple Mount is in our hands* is still a rippling echo in the heart of every Jew. The pictures of Yitzhak Rabin, Moshe Dayan and Uzi Narkis, entering the Old City through the Lion Gate, became a cornerstone in the history of Israel, Jerusalem and the Jewish psyche forever.

* * *

Naima and Moshe, now living in Holon, still yearned for their home in the Jewish Quarter, where they lived most of their lives. They belonged to an elite group of Jewish families who had property in the Jewish Quarter. They were not only anxious to return to their old home but also to realize their dream to be buried in their plot on the Mount of Olives Cemetery. As riots, pogroms and killing continued in the Old City, Moshe and Naima moved their growing family to a neighbourhood outside of the walls, as did other Jewish families. That was just before the Jordanian Legion besieged Jerusalem. This historic victory meant, for Naima and Moshe, that they could finally claim ownership and return to their old home in the Jewish Quarter.

"This is a miracle," said Naima to Moshe. "We are going to return."

"Who knows if our home still exists? Perhaps they destroyed it as they did with the synagogues."

"We have to go! As soon as possible."

"Yes," said Moshe. "We also need to find out what happened to our olive grove behind the tomb of Rachel in Bethlehem. Remember our picnics where we used to collect the ripe olives and deliver them to the Silwan Valley. What was his name? The one who pressed the olives and produced olive oil for us?"

"Of course, I remember our olive grove. In 1928, you bought it to impress my father."

"What do you mean, 'to impress your father'?"

"My father used to encourage all of us to own land. He used to say: *A Jew without a piece of land in the Holy land is worthless.* Even though the only land he ever bought were the grave plots on the Mount of Olives, he repeatedly emphasized the importance of owning land. That reminds me: We have to visit my father's grave."

"Oh, yes. I wonder what happened to the olive tree that I planted beside his grave on the day we buried him.

"Yes, I remember...in 1936."

"You better find all the old papers," said Moshe.

"What papers?"

"The *Kushans*. The deeds given to us before our wedding in 1928 by the British authorities that proves ownership of our home in the Jewish Quarter, proves that the olive grove is ours, our grave plot at the cemetery is ours and our store in the Mamila Market, too."

"I wonder where they are."

"You better find them and also the papers from 1934 or 1935."

"What happened then?"

"Don't you remember, we went with your father to the

Mount of Olives Cemetery and paid the Jewish authorities for your parents' two grave plots, and ours as well."

"Are you sure we still have them?"

"I gave them to you immediately after the burial of your father."

"To tell you the truth, Moshe, I have no idea where they are."

"Please, Naima, open all those hidden shoe boxes and go through the papers. You'll find them."

"This reminds me that my mother, who died in 1948, was not buried beside my father on the Mount of Olives. The Jordanians occupied it then. Now that the Mount of Olives is in our hands, we need to move her from the Givat Shaul Cemetery to the plot next to my father's. When do you want to go?"

"What about tomorrow?"

"Tomorrow is fine."

Naima picked up the phone and dialed her daughter's number: "Hello, Malka."

"Hello, Ima, how are you and Abaa?" said Malka.

"We are fine," said Naima and continued. "We want to go to Jerusalem tomorrow morning and you are the only one who has a car. We'll wait for you at 7 a.m."

"Ima," said Malka with an apology. "I can't tomorrow. I have to be at the university and besides, the roads to Jerusalem will be jammed. Why don't we wait until next week?"

"Sweetie, I'm not going to hear any excuses.

"Ima! I'm living in Ashkelon, remember? With all the morning traffic, I can't make it to Holon by 7 a.m."

"Of course you can. We will be waiting for you at 7 a.m. sharp." And she hung up.

Although Malka showed up as ordered, her mother

complained: "What a waste of time. We were waiting for you since 6 a.m. Let's move."

Her parents squeezed into her mini Fiat and sat with their knees pressed against their chests. Her father was in the front, her mother in the back with a basket loaded with food and drinks.

Driving her elderly parents to Jerusalem that day was a nightmare—a nightmare they endured with grace. With high expectation, Moshe repeatedly said with excitement: "What an historic day."

Naima responded: "Thank God, we are alive to see it."

Moshe, overwhelmed, began humming: "*Vetechezena Ainainu... Ainainu... Ainainu... Ainainu.*"

Although the road to Jerusalem was jammed and the traffic slow, the crowd was joyous and friendly. By the time Malka reached the entrance to the Arab village of Abu-Gaush, the cars were still bumper-to-bumper. The road from Holon to Jerusalem, which usually takes about 1 ? hours, took over eight that day.

People from all around the country flocked in hordes with one single desire: to see with their own eyes, to touch with their own hands, to pray and to kiss with their own lips, the Wall—the Kotel. Families, young and old, orthodox and secular, Ashkenazi and Sephardic, came to express their gratitude for the liberation of Jerusalem. No matter the jammed traffic, they felt an indescribable motivation to be together: to enjoy collectively the realization of an old dream. A young soldier happened to be looking for a lift to Jerusalem. *Kol Ha Kavod, Kol Ha Kavod,* people cheered him.

At around noon that day, Malka reached the centre of Abu-Gaushe. A middle-aged policeman, sweating, stood helpless in the gridlock. "I have never seen such traffic, crazy, maddening!" he vented in apology to the aggravated drivers. A high-ranking army officer appeared from nowhere, surveyed the area and took charge. Ten minutes later, the tangled congestion gradually loosened and cars started to move. As Malka drove out of the village, her mother suddenly declared: "I need to go the bathroom."

"Ima!" said Malka, "I just managed to get out of this mess—I can't return now."

"Let's walk," said Moshe. Malka parked her car on the shoulder and walked with her parents back to the restaurant at the top of the hill.

Hungry people inside the crowded restaurant stood impatiently in line beside each table. "We've never ever seen so many people here, non-stop day and night," said one of the Arab waiters in a hurry, hoisting a large tray loaded with food above his head. To clear his path through the hungry crowd, he elbowed right and left, ignoring their complaints, manoeuvring like a well-trained acrobat.

The line-up beside the washrooms was so long, it took Naima a half an hour to return, complaining: "Disgusting. Terribly dirty." On their way back to the car, they saw a slim bearded man walking on the edge of the highway, carrying in one hand a Torah scroll wrapped like a baby in white cotton and in the other, an open psalm book from which he quietly recited.

Moshe called to him: "Hey, Mister! Where are you going?"

"To Jerusalem."

"Walking?"

"Yes, I couldn't find a ride. I will do anything to get to Jerusalem, even walk."

"There are buses."

"There is no room in them, either."

"How did you get to Abu Goush?"

"An Arab truck driver gave me a lift from the Tel Aviv market, where he loaded fruit and vegetables to be delivered to Abu Goush."

Malka turned to the old man: "Why don't you join us?"

"God bless you. God bless you. You really could carry me with my Torah to Jerusalem?"

"Yes," said Malka, "get in." He climbed in the back seat with Moshe, both holding the Torah scroll on their laps, and her mother, squeezed with the picnic basket in the front.

"What's your name?" asked Moshe.

"Yechiel, but everyone calls me Yichye."

"Where do you come from?"

"From Yemen, Sanaa."

"I meant, where do you live in Israel?"

"Oh, oh! I am from Kfar Sabaa.

"What do you do there?"

"I am the Gabai of our Yeminite synagogue."

"Yichye, why are you carrying this Torah scroll?"

"It is a long story, very long," said Yichye humbly.

"We have plenty of time."

"Well..." After a long pause, Yichye said: "My parents, bless their memory, before they died in Sanaa, I mean in Yemen, they commissioned a Sofer in Aden to scribe this Torah. My father, on his deathbed, asked me to make three promises. First, to leave Yemen and go to Eretz Israel, the Holy Land. Second, to make sure that this Torah scroll will be donated to the Kotel Synagogue. The third promise I made was to purchase grave plots for my family at the Mount of Olives Cemetery. My first promise was fulfilled. The second one will be, too, and with God's help, I will get the grave plots for my family. Only then can I die in peace."

When Malka finally reached West Jerusalem, she found the

traffic snailing through the Jaffa Road and got stuck again beside the Mahane - Yehuda Market.

"Where shall we go first?" Malka asked.

"To the Kotel to pray," said Moshe. "It's been more than 20 years since I last prayed there.

"Me, too," jumped Yichye. "That's the only place that I want to go.

"I want to go to the Mount of Olives first," said Naima, "to visit my father's grave.

"Right now?" Moshe asked.

"Yes, and I also want to see our home in the Jewish Quarter."

"What about our olive grove in Bethlehem?" said Moshe.

"In this terrible traffic?" said Malka. "I don't think we have enough time to visit everything. It is already 3 p.m. If you want to return to Holon tonight, it will be impossible to see everything.

"We have enough time."

"Perhaps we should give up the olive grove and the cemetery, and focus only on the Kotel and your home in the Jewish Quarter," Malka suggested.

"I need to see my father's grave today," Naima insisted.

"No way, no way!" interrupted Moshe. "I have to show Malka the Lion's Gate."

"Today? The Lion's Gate? As if we have nothing else to do!"

"Yes. Since you were a child, Malka, remember the day we buried your grandfather. I wanted to show it to you, but you were asleep."

"Why is it so important? We could see the Gate some other time." Malka asked.

"No, now. It will only take a few minutes. It is important. First, because through this gate the Israeli soldier liberated the Old City and second, the lions engraved above the gate symbolize the Kingdom of Yehuda."

"Oh, yes, yes!" said Yichye, "The Bible mentions many times that lions are our king's symbol."

"I don't think so," said Malka.

"What do you mean?" said her father, annoyed.

"Legend has it that the lions on both sides of the gate were engraved by the Ottoman Sultan, Suleman the Magnificent."

"So what?" said Moshe.

"Suleman the Magnificent is the one who built the present walls, between 1536 to 1541. He was a devout Muslim; the last thing on his mind was engraving Jewish symbols. This is an historical fact."

"Why would a Muslim sultan use lions as his symbol?" asked Moshe.

"Your father," said Yichye, "is right. The lions mentioned in the *tanach* are Jewish."

"It's true," replied Malka, "that the lions are mentioned in the Bible, but the Jews have no exclusive ownership of them. Throughout history, many gentiles, kings, kingdoms and tribes used the lion as their emblem. They were not Jews."

"Nonsense, nonsense," said Moshe sarcastically. "Tell me something, Malka. Why exactly did Suleman the Magnificent decide to carve lions on the gate?"

"Legend has it that Suleman The Magnificent had a dream that warned him that he would be devoured by lions if he didn't build a wall around Jerusalem to protect its citizens from Christian invaders. So he built the walls and expressed his gratitude by carving four lions above the gate."

"I don't believe this," said Moshe.

"Abaa, you are free to believe any myth you choose, but historical facts are unchangeable."

Driving through the narrow road, circling the outside of

the Old City walls was slow. Malka was trying to manoeuvre, taking short cuts like other drivers, to no avail. Her parents and Yichye, who were squeezed into the mini Fiat, began to show signs of impatience. Finally, they reached the square facing the Lion's Gate. Thousands of people pushed and shouted to reach the Gate.

"I can't park here," said Malka. "What should we do?"

"Why don't you leave us here," said Moshe, "and come back in half an hour to pick us up."

"Abaa, I don't think so. It's going to take you more than half an hour to reach the gate and I don't know how long it will take me to return."

"Please, Mrs. Malka, let me out," said Yichye. "I will find my way to the Kotel. God bless you for the lift." Her parents left, too. About a half an hour later, Malka, still stuck in the traffic, saw her parents with Yichye return with long faces.

"Too crowded, too crowded!" said Yichye.

"Unfortunately, we were not able to reach the Lion's Gate," said Moshe.

"We'll come later," said Naima. "Let's move on!"

"To where?"

"To the Dunge Gate, close to the Kotel."

The traffic situation at the Dunge Gate was much worse. "You let us out here and wait," said Moshe. "All I need is to touch the wall, pray and stick this letter into it."

While Malka was stuck inside the car watching the crowd shoving and pushing towards the Gate, her parents and Yichye were swallowed into the crowd. Half an hour later, her parents returned, complaining: "This is impossible. We could not get in here, either. There is an army checkpoint, and they only allow people with special permits in. The line-up is so long that even with the permit, it would take a few hours to get through the Gate."

"Where do we get the permit?" asked Malka.

"They said that we could get it at City Hall in West Jerusalem, but even there, I was told that people have been lined-up since dawn. Perhaps, we could pick them up tomorrow morning."

"This means that we are staying in Jerusalem overnight?"

"Malka, we have no choice," said her father.

"I'm not staying. So, where do we go now?"

"Let's get out of this mess first," said Moshe, "and then to the Jaffa Gate."

"Why the Jaffa Gate?" asked Naima.

"From there," said Moshe, "through the Armenian Quarter, it's a short walk to the Jewish Quarter. Don't you want to see our home?"

"Yes," said Naima, "but this will take us a few hours and I want to see my father's grave today."

"Here is my plan," said Moshe. "From the Jaffa Gate, we will walk through the Jewish Quarter, see our home, go down to the Kotel, exit the Dunge Gate, and that road will lead us straight to the Mount of Olives Cemetery. From there, it is very close to the Lion's Gate. If we have enough time, we can even go to our olive grove in Bethlehem. What do you say?"

"It is already 4 p.m. I am so confused. Please decide where you want to go?" whimpered Malka.

An agitated policeman pounded on Malka's Fiat, ordering her to move on. "Tell me," Malka turned to him, "could we park beside the Jaffa Gate and enter the Jewish Quarter?"

"I don't think so," said the policeman. "The parking area beside the Jaffa Gate is worse than here. The Gate is locked anyway."

"Why is the gate closed?"

"The authorities need some time to put everything in

order. Only people who live inside are allowed in."

"We used to live there," said Moshe. "We have a home in the Jewish Quarter."

"When was the last time you were there?"

"About 22 years ago."

"That's what everyone says. Do you have a permit?"

"No."

"How do you know your home is still standing?"

"We don't know. That's why we want to get in?"

"Don't waste your time. They are not going to let you in unless you have a permit."

While moving her car, Malka turned to her parents, "Where do I go now?"

"Straight to the Mount of Olives," said Naima with a sense of relief.

Excitedly, Malka turned her car around out of the traffic jam and drove down the slope to the Kidron Valley. A stone wall along the right side of the road fenced in the Mount of Olives Cemetery. People walked freely in and out of the cemetery gates. "Which gate leads to Sabaa's grave?" asks Malka.

"I don't really remember," said Naima. "The last time we went to his grave, I believe, was in 1945. I think it was by the southern gate."

"We are beside the southern gate right now," said Malka.

"I think," said Moshe, "it was from the northern gate."

"No," said Naima, "now I remember. It was through this gate. Remember when we came to bury him in 1935, the carriages parked beside those pine trees."

"I don't think so," said Moshe. "First, it was in 1936, now we are 1967, 31 years later. Those pine trees look much younger. Besides, I remember tall cypress trees."

"I'm telling you, it is here. Malka, let us out, find parking and come join us. We are going to climb up to that upper section, see?" Her parents left the car and started to climb. Naima turned to Moshe. "Do you see those stone walls crossing the cemetery all the way around?"

"Yes."

"They divide the cemetery into lower, middle and upper levels."

"Naima, I know!"

"You see that one up there at the very top? That's where my father is buried."

"Naima! I know!"

Naima climbed through the lower and the middle sections, while Moshe stood and examined the devastation around. Naima, full of energy, continued to climb to the upper level, yelling: "Moshe, where are you?"

By the time Malka entered the gate, her parents were already in the upper section, scattered amongst hundreds of other people searching for the graves of their loved ones. Finally, Malka reached the middle level. She stood for a moment to catch her breath and to watch her parents in amazement. They were approaching their 70's, always complaining about pain here, pain there, but today on this mountain, they were like overactive children, full of energy, jumping, climbing between the grey rocks and graves. From a distance they seemed possessed by a spirit who took over their bodies and turned them into ecstatic hovering shadows.

Malka continued to climb and sweat. Her parents disappeared over the horizon; they were nowhere to be seen. The devastating landscape disturbed Malka: ruined rubble, desecration and destruction where ever she looked. Many tombstones were missing, many fallen into rubble, sunk into mounds of earth, many scattered face down on the path, broken, damaged scratched and beaten. Only a few tombstones stood upright the way they were erected years earlier.

An old man stood beside a double tombstone. Malka remarked: "You seem happy."

"Yes, I feel lucky! I found my parent's tombstone."

"Your parent's tombstone was saved? I wonder why it survived?"

"It is too large and heavy to be moved by donkeys."

Beside another of the saved tombstones, a group of Hasidic men dressed in black recited the *kaddish*. Not far from them, an old lady knelt, cling to her husband's gravestone, sobbing: "Take me, take me with you, my love. Save me from my misery."

Hundreds of people were scattered on the vast mountain. Young and old, families, couples, singles, helplessly searched for the graves that once existed. Disappointed, they threw their wilted flowers and candles into the garbage and, upset, they left. A lady standing close to Malka said: "How could we find graves without the tombstones?"

"I don't know," said Malka, and kept climbing. She could not find her parents anywhere. The setting sun had chosen a special position in the sky to say farewell before going to sleep. Behind the Old City walls, the sun, just before sinking, brushed the surviving tombstone peaks with a whispered caress: "Good night, spirits. See you tomorrow morning."

Gradually, people started to climb down and exit the gates. Malka wondered what happened to her parents. Unexpectedly, from the mountaintop, she recognized her mother's excited voice: "Here it is! Here! Here! Moshe! Come! I found my father's grave!"

Malka heard her father's disappointed response: "No, that's not the one. We didn't bury him here. Don't you remember, I planted an olive tree next to his grave? I don't see it."

"Maybe," answered Naima, "they cut it. This mountain used to be full of olive trees. I don't see any now."

"And beside, Naima, where is his tombstone? I don't see it."

Malka caught up to her parents: "Did you find Sabaa's tomb?"

"I'm not sure," said Naima, "it is supposed to be here."

Aggravated, the three of them stood silently. Malka said quietly: "It's almost dark. We have to go."

On their way down, disillusioned and exhausted, they passed by a small stone house surrounded by thorny weeds that penetrated the cracks in the wall. A bearded man of unidentifiable age, wearing a long black coat, holding a kerosene lamp was locking the door.

Naima stopped and asked him: "Who are you?"

"I am the cemetery guardian. A volunteer."

"We were not able to find my father's grave."

"Yes, yes, I know. It's difficult, very difficult," he mumbled. "Many tombstones were stolen by the Arabs to build their homes."

"Are you saying we will never find my father's grave?"

"No, I didn't say that. All I'm saying is with God's help, we will."

"How could God help us find our missing tombstone?"

"The tombstone, we might not find, but the grave, we will."

"How?"

"Since the Turkish Ottomans, every grave here has been documented; documented with details about the section, the level, the row, the number in each row and even the name of the deceased and his living family. All this information has been kept in the yearly books."

"Where are those books?"

"In 1947, before the Jordanians took over, we managed to retrieve them for safekeeping. Now that the cemetery is in our hands, all the books are back here in this office."

"Could you please check where my father's grave is?"

"Sorry, not now. It's too late. I need to go down, lock the gates and stay overnight at the mountain. Why don't you come tomorrow morning?"

"Why do you have to stay overnight?"

"To protect the cemetery from thieves."

"Thieves?"

"Oh, yes, thieves. Even yesterday night, a group of Arab men broke through the gate up there, entered with their mules and started to load tombstones that they unearthed a few nights earlier. The fact that the mountain is in our hands does not prevent them from stealing."

"What did you do?"

"We called the police and they arrested them. Concerning your father's grave, come tomorrow and I'll do my best. With a small donation, I could also prepare a *minyan* to read the *kaddish*. All you need to do is ask for me—my name is Yosel."

"We'll be here tomorrow," said Naima."

With new hope, Malka and her parents left the cemetery. It was almost 8 p.m. In the car, Naima opened the basket and finally served sandwiches and drinks—their first meal that day. A new argument erupted.

Malka turned to her parents: "Why did you tell Yosel that we are coming tomorrow? Aren't we supposed to return to Holon tonight?"

"Yes, we are returning to Holon tonight, and tomorrow morning you'll drive us back."

"I can't drive back to Holon in this kind of traffic and

return to Jerusalem tomorrow," said Malka. "Why don't we stay here with your sister in Nahalat Shiva overnight?"

"No, no way," said a resolute Naima. "I haven't seen her in over 20 years. I will never forgive her for what she has done."

"Naima, please! This is not the time to dwell on the past."

"Moshe, you'd better shut up. You forgot that she didn't bother to tell me that my mother was dead. I discovered coincidentally a year later."

"Naima, perhaps I should remind you that it was wartime. It wasn't that simple."

"Moshe, you are a genius in finding excuses. A war doesn't justify her behaviour. She totally ignored me, excluded me, took everything from my mother and didn't even show me her will."

"It's 9 p.m. already and I'm tired," said Malka. "Perhaps we should find a hotel?"

By 10:30 p.m. Malka returned from the last hotel in the area without any results. In the car, both her parents had dozed off. She touched their shoulders and woke them up. "All the hotels are all fully booked," she told her sleepy parents. "Even the hotel lobbies are jammed with mattresses. It seems like the whole population of Israel is spending this night in Jerusalem. Look at those people there on the sidewalks crumpled into their sleeping bags."

"Well we could sleep here in the car."

"Moshe, are you crazy? In this box? My body is aching. I'd rather sleep in the street."

"I know what," said Malka. "Wait here. I'm going to call a friend of mine in Kibutz Kiryat – Anavim, or a friend in Rehavia." When Malka returned, her father was snoring.

Her sleepy mother asked: "What happened?"

"There is no answer at Kiryat – Anavim and my friends in

Rehavia have family staying who came from places all around the country. They have no room for us."

"I know what," said Naima, "let's go to our old friend Senora Samuha, in the Nahalat Zion neighbourhood. She undoubtedly will be excited to see us. What do you think, Malka?"

"Let's try."

Moshe woke up: "Naima, are you totally out of your mind? It's almost 11 at night. We can't disturb her this late."

"Moshe, I was a very close friend with her. She came to Holon many summers to visit with her five daughters and I am absolutely sure that she'll be glad to see us."

"Ima, I remember her daughter, Shulamit. She was my best friend at elementary school. I wonder what happened to her."

At 11:30 that night, Senora Samuha and her two unmarried daughters, in their nightgowns, sleepy, rubbing their eyes, opened the door. Immediately Naima, Moshe and Malka were engulfed in overwhelming joy: excited hugging, kissing, pinching and jumping. As if this was not enough, one of them rushed to wake up all the neighbours and invite them to come greet the unexpected visitors. Gradually, the whole neighbourhood rushed in, wearing bathrobes over their pyjamas. In the midst of all the joking and laughing, the sisters served the women Turkish coffee and to cheer up the sleepy men, they served Arake, followed by endless trays of pastries and all sorts of baked nuts and seeds. Although the beds were ready, no one went to sleep that night. The few dozen people who were crowded into the living room enthusiastically shared stories and tales about this historic war, and made plans for the new future of Israel and new relations with the Arab world, in prosperity and peace. Everyone was certain that peace between Israelis and Arabs

MASONS

was at hand. Above all, each had the perfect plan for the revival, rebuilding and reconstruction of the Jewish Quarter.

At dawn, while Senora Samuha returned from the kitchen laughing, her daughters served breakfast. Gradually, the neighbours went back to their homes and Senora Samuha declared: "Here is my plan. I have spoken with a friend of mine who works at City Hall and he has already prepared the permits for you, the ones you need to get into the Old City. This will save you hours of standing in line. All you need to do is to go to Jerusalem City Hall and ask for Sason. Everyone knows him. He will give you the permits."

"Senora Samuha, you are an angel!" said Moshe.

"Now Malka, you leave your car here and return in the evening to pick it up," Senora Samuha said. "I suggest you stay here at least another night. We're going to have a big party."

"How do we get to the City Hall?" asked Malka.

"I have already called for a taxi. He will take you. From there, it is a short walk to the Jaffa Gate, where you can see your home in the Jewish Quarter. It's a short walk again to the Kotel, which is not far from the cemetery. What do you think?"

"It's a excellent idea," said Malka. "There is no way I'll find parking in that area."

A honking taxi outside stopped their conversation.

At the City Hall, Sason welcomed them with the permits, and he reminded Naima that when they were kids they played in the same neighbourhood and her parents were friends with his.

They picked up another taxi to the Jaffa Gate and, to their surprise, with the permit, they were allowed to enter without any problem. They walked through the familiar streets of the Armenian Quarter.

"I don't see any changes," said Moshe. It looks like if the whole neighbourhood was frozen in time."

"Yes," said Naima, "it looks exactly like 22 years ago. I wonder if all our Armenian friends are still here. We should surprise them with a visit one day."

Entering the Jewish Quarter was different. It was like walking through a bombed city; the synagogues were in ruins, destroyed. Most of the houses were in rubble mixed with garbage. Dirty, emaciated, sick dogs strayed everywhere, sniffing for food. What used to be clean stone paved alleys now were covered with mounds of dirty earth, stone and debris.

"I am all lost," said Moshe. "I can't find any of our synagogues. Not even my synagogue Yohannan Ben Zakai—like it never existed."

Here and there, arched dark tunnels that in the past led a clear path to back courtyards were now junked with debris. Arab children played in the rubble. "Devastating," Naima mourned, then asked one of the children: "What street is this?"

"We call it Harat - El - Yahud."

"Really," said Moshe. "This is Harat - El - Yahud? I don't recognize anything here."

"Unbelievable," Naima said repeatedly while searching for familiar reference points. Surprised that she might have found the entrance to their courtyard, she called: "Moshe! Moshe! Come here!"

Moshe approached Naima: "Oh, yes, this is the one."

Malka also surprised said: "Oh, yes. I remember this cool arched tunnel, especially on the hot summer days.

Hopping over mounds of garbage and dirt, they passed through the tunnel and entered the courtyard. To their surprise, the courtyard's stone pavement was clean and shiny.

The water well was exactly where it used to be. A few old wrinkled buckets stood beside the well. The stony stairs on the left leading to their home on the roof was still there.

"Something is missing," said Naima. "The garden on the roof, the one that you loved, Moshe, has disappeared."

"Yes, I can see. They replaced it with two additional rooms."

Around the courtyard, like before, were four rooms at the east and four rooms at the west but the three rooms that used to be in the south had been replaced with new toilets and bathrooms. The communal kitchen under the stairs, which used to be opened, is now closed in.

"Malka," said Moshe, "do you see that room on the right side on the roof? That's where you were born. That's where we lived until about 1940. Your kindergarten used to be not far from here on the same street."

"It seems like people are living here. I hear them talking inside," said Malka.

A boy of about seven years old, with some hesitation, approached them. "Are you looking for someone?" he asked in Arabic.

"Yes," replied Naima in Arabic. "We want to know who lives up there."

The boy pointed up: "You mean there on the roof? That's where my family lives. Ibrahim is my father."

Moshe was startled: "Ibrahim? Which one?"

"Ibrahim Iben Suleman. Suleman, my grandfather, died a year ago, but my grandmother Zahra lives down there. Let me call her."

Moshe turned to Naima whispering: "I think that this is Suleman's family—the one who used to be my helper in the Mamila Market. You remember, Naima. You used to be a good friends with his wife Zahra until he tried to kill me."

"Yes," said Malka, "I remember Ibrahim. I used to play with him beside this water well. By the way, I had a big crush on him."

"I didn't know that, Malka. You never told me," said Naima.

"You women are unbelievable. This Suleman tried to run me over with his truck; he broke my two legs. I was in hospital for almost a year and you are talking about your childhood crush?"

"I'm sorry, Abaa. I remember you were in the hospital, but I never knew Suleman tried to kill you. When was it?"

"When we moved to Nahalat Zion. I started a new business, Suleman asked me to leave him my coffee shop in the Mamila Market so he could continue to sell coffee and tea. We agreed that he would pay me rent of five lirot per month. For over ten years he never paid a penny—not a single penny. Like this was not enough, I had to pay from my own pockets the taxes, the roof repairs, the plumbing and for the lawyer to force him out. He still refused to leave. So in 1945, I had no choice but to take him to court."

"What happened in court?" Malka asked.

"Naima interfered: "Don't ask him. It's a long story."

"Did he compensate you?" asked Malka.

"No, that's when he tried to kill me."

"You mean, he never paid you?"

"No, never. The Jordanians in 1947 took over the east side of the city. In the war of 1948, Jerusalem was divided and my file against Suleman probably found its way to Jordan. By the way, Naima, did you bring the *koushan* deed for our store in the Mamila Market? Perhaps one of our children could use it. What about you Malka?"

"No way," Malka said, "I'm not interested."

All of a sudden, they heard a woman howling, whining

and wailing: *Ya—Mahabubi, Ya—Mahabubi, Ta Alu—Hon, Ta Alu*! My beloved. My beloved. Come here, come. They turned around. Zahra, fat with deeply ploughed hands and face appeared wearing a flowery dress and a silky red beaded headscarf. She rushed towards Naima with open arms: *Ta Ali—Hon Ya Ichti, Ya Aini Ta Ali—Hon,* come here my sister, my eye, come here, hugging and kissing Naima all over. In a few minutes, neighbouring women and their children brought tables and chairs for Moshe, Naima and Malka. At the helm, orchestrating what she called a big hafla celebration, was Zahra. Amina, Ibrahim's wife, served coffee, sweets, salted pastry, baked nuts and seeds. Excited Zahra announced: "Have something to eat."

"No, no," said Moshe. "We came just for a few minutes."

In the midst of this uproar and mayhem, Zahra pulled up a chair and squeezed herself between Naima and Moshe: "Why don't you stay here overnight so tomorrow evening, we will have a real *hafla* in your honour? All your Arab friends will come. Believe me, they will be extremely happy to see you after all these years. What do you say, huh?"

Moshe, who was not in the mood for a *hafla*, said seriously: "Zahra, tell me, when did you move here? You know that this courtyard belonged to Jewish families."

"*Ay ya ya yi,*" said Zahra holding Moshe's shoulders like an old intimate friend. "*Ya-ruhi* Musa. As you know, in 1948, after our great victories, the Jordanian Legion was determined to destroy the Jewish Quarter. The entire Jewish population vanished, leaving the Jewish Quarter empty. To save your homes, we immediately moved in."

"To save our homes?"

"Yes, the Jordanian destroyed everything, like they did with your synagogues, except the homes where Arabs lived. At the beginning, all our children and their families lived in the rooms downstairs. Suleman and I, bless his soul, lived in your room on the roof. When our children's families grew, some moved out of the Old City, so we rented all the rooms here except the one I'm living in and the one up there occupied by Ibrahim. Once that room became too small for him and his eight children, he built, as you can see, two extra rooms."

"Zahra, are you telling me that you collected rent from these Jewish properties for over 20 years?"

"Yes," said Zahra, "why not? It's our property, legally registered with the Jordanian authorities in Aman. We've paid taxes all these years and you, Musa should be grateful; we saved your property. If other Jewish owners return to their homes, they will find nothing."

"Grateful for what, Zahra? Are you going to pay me 20 years rent, for our room up there?"

"Of course not. First, we built extra rooms and a special modern bathroom and kitchen. Actually, if it were empty, the Jordanians would have flattened it. Now, if you want to return and live here, you have to compensate me."

"Yes, we want to return. How much?"

"It is not that simple. You have to pay us enough to replace this land, the 11 rooms, the new toilets and bathrooms and kitchen. We need to buy something similar somewhere else."

"Please tell me, how much—just for our room on the roof, Zahra?"

"I don't know. I have to consult with an agent and a lawyer. It is very complex and beside, look there. Do you see a tomb?"

"Whose tomb is this?"

"This is Suleman. On his deathbed, he insisted on being buried here."

"Buried...here? You have your own cemeteries. Why

would a Muslim want to be buried on Jewish land?"

"Don't ask me," said Zahra. "This was Suleman's wish."

"Look, Zahra," said Naima, "all we want is to return to our home—to die on this holy land. The rooms down here do not belong to us. They have different owners."

Zahra, slightly angry, clearly emphasized: "Look, I am not going to bother with ten or 12 owners. I want to sell everything in one single deal. If you want your home back, find the other owners and then we will talk. In the meantime, if I can get a good deal, I'm going to sell."

Ibrahim, who arrived through the dark tunnel, disrupted the tense conversation. He joined them, and with a surprised yet timid smile he quietly asked: "Is this you, Malka? Or am I dreaming?" He extended his hand. "Good to see you again. It has been so many years."

Malka blushed: "Good to see you, Ibrahim." Amina, with burning eyes, carefully examined each of their moves.

Ibrahim turned to his wife: "Amina, where are the children?"

"Ibrahim *ya eini*," she said softly, "you came early today, they are still in school."

"Oh, yes, someone told me at work that very important guests came to our home. So I rushed to see who."

Moshe, anxious, turned to Naima: "We better go."

"Wait, wait," begged Zahra, "lunch will be ready soon." They ignored her invitation and left.

Outside, clinging to one another, Moshe, Naima and Malka walked down the broken stairs, hopping above rubble, helping each other on their way to the Kotel. Crowds impatiently stood in lines under the burning sun, waiting their turn to enter the Kotel alley. Thirsty and dehydrated, they yearned for the privilege to only touch the wall. Someone yelled: "Moshe! Moshe! Come here! I reserved this place in line for you!"

"Oh," said Moshe, "Yichye."

Yichye hushing them, squeezed Moshe, Naima and Malka into the line. Grumbling, Naima said: "How long will it take up to reach the Kotel?"

"Only a few hours," said Yichye amusingly. "I've been waiting in line since I left you last night. I was afraid to lose my turn so, like a horse, I slept standing up."

"I'm going to faint," said Naima.

"Please, Naima," said Moshe, "all I want is to touch the wall for a minute."

"You go touch the wall," insisted Naima. "Malka and I are going to the Mount of Olives Cemetery."

"Wait! Wait!" cried Moshe while running after them.

Outside the Dunge Gate, not a single taxi could be found so they walked down the slope to the Kidron Valley and entered the Mount of Olives Cemetery through the south gate. They climbed to Yosel's office, but he was busy with an old man searching for his parents' tombs. "Please wait inside the office where it's shady. I'll be back soon."

Inside the office was an old wooden table and a few chairs. The shelves all around were loaded with old fat faded black books. When Yosel arrived, the first question he asked was: "What's your father's name?"

"Mordechai Alafi," said Naima.

"When did he die?"

"In 1935," she said.

"No," said Moshe, "in 1936."

"You don't expect me to check the books of more than one date?" He pulled out a large black book, where, on its spine, was written in white '1935.' While flipping through the pages, he asked: "What month and what day?"

"It was just before Passover," said Moshe. "We don't

96

remember the exact date."

"Oh, here it is! I found Mordechai Alafi! I know exactly where his grave is. Follow me." Instead of climbing to the upper level, Yosel descended to the lower one.

"Excuse me, Yosel," said Naima, "this is not where my father is buried. He should be up there."

"What was the year he was buried, you said?"

"1936," said Moshe.

"You told me '35. According to the book of 1935, Mordechai Alafi should be down here. Perhaps it is someone else."

"Yes," said Naima, "we had four Mordechais in my family. All of them are Alafis."

They walked back to the office. In the 1936 volume, Yosel found a second Mordechai Alafi.

"This one," said Yosel, "was buried in the upper level in the last row. Follow me." They reached the area where Moshe and Naima visited a day earlier. Mordechai's tombstone was nowhere to be found.

"Here, exactly here, is where you father is buried," said Yosel.

"Impossible," said Moshe, "I planted an olive tree next to the grave and I don't see any sign of it." Yosel brushed the earth with his foot and turned to Moshe.

"See this tree stump? They cut it."

"This couldn't be my father's grave," said Naima.

"Why?" asked Yosel.

"The grave beside my father was purchased for my mother. It should be empty and it's not. She is buried in the Givat-Shaul Cemetery because during the war, we had no access to the Mount of Olives. We want to bring her here as we promised. Who is buried in her plot beside my father?"

"I don't know," said Yosel. "I'm confused."

"Yes," said Moshe. "I am puzzled, too. Look, Yosel, I also purchased the plots beside Mordechai for my wife and myself. As you can see two other people are buried in our plots."

"Possible, possible," said Yosel. "During the war in 1947 and '48, many mistakes were made. As the tombstones are missing, the only way I can know is by looking at the book of 1947."

At the office, Yosel discovered that buried beside Mordechai was someone by the name of Yehuda Mualem. Buried beside Mualem was a couple from the Mizrahi family, who was killed by a Jordanian sniper in 1947. "I can't believe this," said Moshe. "Naima? Remember Yehuda Mualem and his wife Yudit? They lived beside Yohannan Ben Zakai Synagouge. They owned the building with the kindergarten where Malka used to go."

"Of course, I remember," said Naima. "We were at their son's wedding, I think in 1946."

"You knew them?" said Yosel.

"Oh yes, very well," said Moshe.

"How come," complained Naima, "Mualem is buried in my mother's plot? And the Mizrahis in ours? I don't understand."

"As I told you before," said Yosel, "during the war of 1947 and '48, many mistakes were made."

"This means," said Naima upset, "that we cannot move my mother here and we need to buy a new plot for ourselves?"

"To tell you the truth," said Yosel, "even if you want to pay for a new plot on this mountain, it's impossible. The authorities decided to keep the empty plots for dignitaries. We are in the process of changing the old regulations."

"What should we do now?" asked Naima upset.

"Order a new tombstone for your father and prepare for a new unveiling. With a minimal donation, I will help you."

"What if we find the old tombstone?"

"I'm afraid you couldn't use it," said Yosel. "It's not kosher."

"What?" said Moshe. "Even a tombstone needs to be kosher?"

"Well, unearthed, desecrated tombstones according to the Jewish custom are considered impure. We call it *tame*. You have to order a new one."

On their way out of the cemetery, they were upset and silent. "I want to go back to Holon," said Naima.

"Naima, don't you want to see the Kotel?"

"No."

"Don't you want to see the Lion's Gate?"

"No."

"Don't you want to see the tomb of Rachel and our olive grove in Bethlehem and our store in Mamila?"

"No," said Naima, "No, no, no! I am fed up. Enough is enough. Let's go home."

* * *

A few weeks later, Malka with two of her girlfriends in Ashkelon decided on Saturday morning to drive to what they remembered as a lush green oasis surrounded by dry, arid desert, Jericho.

After their lunch in Jericho, they shopped. Loaded with delicious well-known Jericho goodies—dates, figs, divine juicy pamelot, and baked nuts—they hit the road back home. Malka drove. "This is unbelievable," said Tovah. "A few weeks earlier, we were at war, killing one another, and now notice how friendly they were; they treated us like royalty."

"Of course, they need our business," said Rachel.

"They gave us great bargains. Don't you think?"

"Yes," said Rachel, "to cover their deep hatred; they lick our asses like Turkish rahat lakum."

In the middle of nowhere, Tovah turned to Malka: "I have to go to the washroom. Could you please stop somewhere?"

"Can't you wait until we cross this deserted area?" said Malka.

"No. I have to go now," said Tovah. "I think I have diarrhea from that mishwi we ate in Jericho."

"Me, too!" said Rachel. Malka parked the car along the road and all of them rushed for cover in the ruins of a deserted Arab village. The roofless huts were surrounded by high prickly weeds and yellow mustard flowers. Black crows circled above. Endless armies of ants marched between the thorny weeds towards their unknown destination. All of a sudden, Rachel's voice pierced the air: "I can't believe this!"

"What! What! What!" responded Tovah, while pulling up her jeans.

"Come here, Tovah!" Rachel said. "Look! Tombstones! Jewish tombstones!"

"So what?" said Tovah.

"What do you mean, 'so what'? These are Jewish tombstones. What are they doing in a desolate Arab village?"

"You're right," said Tovah. I can see more of them here and here and here. They are all engraved in Hebrew letters."

Chaim Ben Jacov
Born in 1911
Died in 1943.

"It seems like Chaim died young," said Rachel. "Here is another one built into the wall."

Devorah
Daughter of Isaac and Lilly

"I can't see her dates; they are covered in mud. Where do you think they came from?"

Malka, who didn't hear them, tangled her hair in a spiderweb as she left the mud hut. She raised her head to push the web away when she noticed a flat marble stone lintel engraved in Hebrew:

Mordechai.
The son of Shlomo and Devorah Alafi.
Born in Baghdad, 1880
Died in Jerusalem, 1936

"Un-be-liveable!" Malka rubbed her eyes in disbelief. "This is un-be-liveable!" Excited, she called Rachel and Tovah. "Look at this!" she pointed.

"Yes," said Rachel, "we saw many other Jewish tombstones over there. Come and see."

"This one is very special to me," said Malka in a pensive tone.

"What do you mean?" said Tovah.

"This is my own grandfather's tombstone."

"No way!" said Tovah.

"Are you kidding?" said Rachel. "How do you know?"

"I know, not only by his name and dates, but there is something else. I remember—the olive tree carved by my uncle *Isaac*. If you look carefully, you will see it partly, here. It was taken from the Mount of Olives Cemetery where he was buried."

* * *

That night, Malka called her parents: "I'll believe it only if I see it," said her mother. Although suspicious, Naima immediately called old Isaac in Jerusalem.

"Isaac," she said, "you carved my father's tombstone. Remember?"

Sleepy and angry, Isaac responded: "Yes, I did. That's why you woke me up in the middle of the night?"

"I'm sorry, Isaac," said Naima, "but my daughter just told me that she found it on the way to Jericho. How would we know it's his?"

"It's very simple," said Isaac while clearing his throat. "Your father asked me on his deathbed to carve an olive tree on his tombstone, which I did. If my olive tree is there, that tombstone undoubtedly is his. And by the way, Naima, I almost finished carving his new tombstone."

"Thank you, thank you so much," said Naima and immediately called Malka in Ashkalon.

"Malka! Did you see the olive tree?"

"What olive tree?"

"The one carved on my father's tombstone?"

"Oh, yes, it is so delicately carved and beautiful."

* * *

About a year later, Naima, Moshe, all their children, grandchildren, friends and neighbours boarded three buses that took them from Holon to the cemetery on the Mount of Olives for the unveiling of Mordechai's new tombstone. At the end of the ceremony, Moshe turned to his guests: "Do you want to see our home in the Jewish Quarter?"

"Yes, of course," everyone raved.

To everyone's disappointment, the Jewish Quarter inside the walls was closed, blocked and unapproachable.

According to the security people at the Jaffa Gate, the Jewish Quarter was flattened, and foundations for the new Quarter were in the process of being dug and built.

"Well," said Moshe, "we could walk down to see our store in the Mamila Market."

"I'm sorry," said the policeman. "The Mamila Market with its land was confiscated by the state and flattened. They are about to build a new shopping centre."

Again disappointed, Moshe came up with a new suggestion: "Why don't we go and have a look at our olive grove behind Rachel's tomb in Bethlehem."

"Yes, yes, yes!" said everyone.

Here, too, an unpleasant surprise awaited them. Their olive grove was circled in barbed wire with large signs warning:

Army Property.
Dangerous Landmine.
Don't Enter.

On their way back to Holon, except Moshe and Naima, everyone in the bus fell asleep.

"Moshe," said Naima, "I feel blessed spending this wonderful day with all our children and grandchildren. How about you?"

"I'm very upset. I feel everyone robbed us: not only of our grave plots but our home in the Jewish Quarter, our store in Mamila and even our olive grove in Bethlehem—all gone, confiscated by the state and no one bothered to inform us. This is unfair. Where is justice?"

"I know, Moshe. I already spoke with a lawyer who specializes in these kind of things."

"And...what did he say?"

"I even showed him all our deeds. He said that after the Six Day War, they are not relevant anymore. The state confiscated everything and there is nothing we can do."

"How could they do that to us?" said Moshe.

"The lawyer suggested that we should see this as a donation to our country."

"A donation? Aren't we paying enough taxes?"

"Moshe," said Naima while caressing his back, "this is one of the prices for our independence."

THE LEATHER VENDOR

THE BABYLON TOWER IN A SANDBOX AT YEMIN-MOSHE PARK

Jerusalem Winds

Winter in Jerusalém, 1937. Early morning, bitter cold. In one hand, five-year-old Yael held her younger sister Devorah's hand, in the other she held two *tik-haochel* lunch boxes. From the Nahalat Tsion neighbourhood, dressed in long, heavy winter coats, wool hats, scarves, gloves and black rubber boots, they climbed up a rocky hill towards Esther's kindergarten at the top. On their right, was what they dreaded the most: the Bet-Mahase courtyard where Yael and Devorah were always afraid to cross. On a normal day, ultra-orthodox boys dressed in black threw stones at them, viciously yelling: '*Shvartze neshume*! Black devil spirit!' Miraculously, to the girls' relief, the boys in black could not be seen anywhere.

The wind...the cruel wind curled, twisted and hurled debris on the path, threatening to separate their hands, tossing them from right to left, pushing them backward and forward like matches in a storm. Torrential rain made the path between the rocks muddy and slippery. Devoid of mercy, the winds beat against their bodies, mischievously grabbing their hats, flinging them like autumn leaves and whirling them into the sky. In Yael's desperate attempt to catch their hats, her hand slipped from her little sister's. The angry wind pushed Devorah to the muddy ground, rolling her down between the rocks. Screaming for Yael: "Help! Help!" she finally landed at the foot of the hill, hidden behind a boulder.

Devorah on the hilltop, clutched a wet, slippery rock and

screamed in crying despair: "Yael! Yael! You promised Ima never to leave my hand! Please don't leave me alone. I'm scared...scared."

Yael pushed herself up. Beaten, bruised, she shook the mud off her coat and climbed up towards Devorah. Shaky and panicked, she called out: "Don't cry, Devorah. Please don't cry. I'm coming..."

They started for Esther's kindergarten again, holding hands tighter. The violent vicious wind renewed its assault. This time it grabbed the lunch boxes, tossed, twisted and banged them far off against the rocks. They too landed at the bottom of the hill. Quivering, Yael ordered: "Devorah, sit down here and wait. Don't move."

"No! No!" exclaimed Devorah. "No! No! No!"

"I have to go," begged Yael, "to get the lunchboxes."

"No! No! No!"

"If I don't," said Yael, "Ima will kill me."

"I wish she would!" said angry Devorah. "If you leave me alone again, I'll tell her!"

"You won't."

"Yes, I will. Just wait and see."

Torn between her duty to retrieve the lunch boxes for fear of her mother or protect her sister, Yael decided to give up on the lunch boxes and stay with her threatening sister. Hand tightly in hand, they continued to climb. Again, without warning, the fierce wind tumbled Devorah down the hill like a ball. The trunk of an old olive tree stopped her from falling farther. Frantically, Yael ran for Devorah, lifting her into a loving embrace and wiped the blood off her cheek with her wet coat sleeve. She kissed Devorah's curly wet hair and held her face between her hands, whimpering: "I love you, Devorah. I am sorry about all this. I will never leave you alone again."

Finally, beaten, tired, scared and soaking wet, they arrived at their kindergarten.

"Why are you late?" Esther asked angrily.

"The wind and the rain beat us down the hill," Yael answered quietly, eyes glued to her dirty boots.

"It's already lunchtime. Where are your lunch boxes?" blamed Esther.

"We lost them on our way. The wind took them," says Yael, sadly.

"You, Yael, go and find them now!" the teacher ordered.

"I'm scared."

"Scared of what?"

"The wind is frightening."

The teacher turned to the children, clapped her hands and declared in a venomous voice:

"Listen children! Did you hear that? Yael is afraid of the wind." The children laughed. Esther turned back to Yael: "Look at you! You can't walk into class with all this dirt and mud. Go home with your sister and tell your mother to come see me tomorrow."

When Yael and Devorah arrived home unexpectedly, their mother was already in an offensive mood. "What happened?" she asked accusingly.

"The teacher told us to return home."

"Why?"

"Because we are dirty."

"Where are your hats?"

"We lost them."

"Where are your lunch boxes?"

"We lost them, too."

"Lost them? How?"

"The wind took them."

"Where are your scarves and gloves?"

"The teacher hung them there to dry. We forgot them at school."

To be the centre of attention, Devorah cried: "Mummy, mummy! Look what Yael did to me!" Showing the bruises on her face, she added: "She beat me and left me alone. Mummy! Mummy! Look at my bleeding bruised knees. It's all Yael's doing."

"Come here, sweetie. Come here," she said hugging and kissing her hair. She carefully examined her bruises and turned to Yael: "Why did you beat your sister? Didn't I tell you that your duty as the elder is to take care of her?"

"I didn't beat her! It was the wind!" exploded Yael.

"The wind? What kind of nonsense is this? You are lying again."

"I am not, I am not lying. You always blame me for things I didn't do. I hate you all."

"You always lie, Yael. Now go back to the kindergarten, pick up the scarves and gloves, and find the hats and the lunch boxes. Don't dare come back home without them."

Crying, Yael left. She fruitlessly searched for a few hours. She couldn't find the hats; the lunch boxes were nowhere to be seen. By the time she reached the kindergarten, it was closed, the gate locked. Frozen, scared and wet, Yael contemplated the consequences of returning home empty-handed. The night fell under the dark clouds. "What now?" she thought.

Unable to face her mother, she sat on a rock in the rain, crying. Face down, she dreamt of a miracle: an angel who will come to her rescue, like the fairy who saved Cinderella from her vicious mother and sisters. She had no idea what time it was. It was simply dark, and probably long after suppertime; her parents were undoubtedly in a deep sleep.

Unexpectedly, a large, dirty, black rubber boot appeared

on the ground below her eyes. She looked up. Staring down at her was an oversized fat, dirty man, wearing tattered wet clothes. He knelt down and looked softly into her eyes.

"Little girl, why are you sitting alone in the rain?" She didn't respond. Instead, she wiped her tears and bowed her head down lower. He lifted her chin up and softly said: "What is it?" Still silent, tears of hope streamed down her face. "Why are you crying?" She remained quiet. "Do you want a candy?" he said in an encouraging voice. She stopped crying; a spark of interest lit her quiet eyes. He gently took her hand in his and said: "Come with me. I have candy at home."

Quietly they walked down the hill, but something was strange; he led her in the opposite direction of her home. Alarmed, she pulled her hand away from his, asking: "Where are we going?"

"We are going to my shack. I promised to give you a candy. Don't you want a candy? Perhaps a hot cup of tea, too."

"I am hungry. I didn't eat all day." She told him about her day's adventures. He hardly listened. While unlocking the door to his wooden shack, he said: "I will make you chicken soup. Do you like chicken soup."

"Do you have bread?"

"Not today, but next time."

They entered the dark shack. He locked the door from the inside and put the key in his pants pocket. He lit a candle, fed some wood and old newspaper into a rusty iron barrel and started a fire. Then, he filled up the kettle with water and placed it on an iron net above the flames. Taking her hand, he led her to the bed under the leaking, cracked window.

"Come here, my child, come here, Yael." Fear crept into her bulging eyes: "How do you know my name."

"I know. I know your whole family. I used to help your father build the terrace above your kitchen roof." He paused, then continued: "You are so beautiful. Let me take off your clothes."

"No, no! I'm not taking off my clothes!" she protested.

"Just to dry them. Don't worry. Don't be afraid. I am a good friend of your father."

Gradually he took her clothes off and hung them beside the fire on a broken chair. Water leaked from the tin roof onto the mattress, splashing about. Yael nervously grabbed the dirty, wet sheet off the bed, wrapped herself and stood beside the mucky mattress. He pulled the bed away from the leaky roof, picked a lollipop from the jar on the shelf and said: "Here is a sucker. Tea will be ready in a few minutes. Let me hold you. Let me warm you up." Yael backed away.

Intently, he removed his pants, tossed them aside, tore the sheet off her body, and squeezed her naked little self between his legs. He held her so tightly she could hardly breathe. He pushed something that she'd never seen between her legs. Something hard, rounded, strong and burning between her thighs.

"No, no! What are you doing? Let me out of here!" she screamed in desperate horror, trying to escape his chaining arms. She failed.

Angrily, he threw her onto the dirty mattress and lay above her like a hairy monkey. He forced her legs open, pushed wildly against her small unknowing body, tearing into her like a sword, one hand blocking her screaming mouth, with the other pushed with burning force. The sound of the rusted bed reminded Yael of the sound from her parent's bedroom at night.

Yael tried to kick him, hit him, beat him or push him away. Useless. He was as heavy as a barrel of rocks. Helpless. Furiously, she freed her right hand from under his body. With all the energy she could muster, she stuck her little fingers into his mouth. Just before his jaws clamped down, she slipped them away and stuck them in his eyes.

"Aiyeeee!" he screamed. "You little devil. Why did you do that?" He rolled his body to the side and wiped the blood from his eyes.

Yael knew this was her only chance. In a split second, she slid from underneath him and fell to the floor. She rushed to the door, but it was locked. He came after her, his face bleeding. He reached for her little feet, but she managed to jump onto the shaky table and throw herself outside through the broken glass window. She fell naked into a mud puddle. Panicked, she frantically stood up and ran forward, ran, ran. His voice behind her bellowed threats: "If you tell your parents, I will kill you, kill you all. I know where you live, you dirty Jews."

Yael continued to run until she realized that she was running farther away from home. "Home," she thought, "I want to go home." The rain showered the mud off her body. When she reached the alley leading to the Bet—Mahase, it was almost dawn. "The people here will stone me if they see me naked," she anxiously thought. She found a tattered, ratty rug in a nearby garbage can and covered herself, then continued towards her neighbourhood.

From a distance, she saw two policemen beside the entrance of her home. One of them held her crying mother in hopes of calming her. Her father stood by like always, quiet and helpless. The policemen's brass buttons gleamed like ominous stars in the rising sun. It dawned on Yael that those policemen probably saw what she did with the fat man and came to arrest her—take her away to prison and kill her for her sin. Her fear swelled into a haunting full sprint—away from home. Haunted, she is still running...running ...running.

* * *

About 30 years later, to be exact, in 1968 after the Six Day War, Yael and her sister Devorah sat on a bench in the shade of the Yemin Moshe Windmill, overlooking the old city. They enjoyed the rose blossoms close by and reminisced about their childhood in the Nahalat-Tsion neighbourhood. Their children played in the sandbox. Hila, Yael's daughter, rushed to her mother, complaining: "Ima, Ima, the Babel Tower that we're building keeps falling. What should we do?"

Yael took Hila back to the sandbox, sat with them and explained: "Children, if you want to build a solid tower, you need to build a large firm foundation, like this, and get it narrower and narrower towards the top, like this, with spiralling steps."

"Why spiralling steps?" asks David, Devorah's son.

"The spiralling steps are needed for the builders to step up on the tower, to continue building it higher and higher."

"Ima, Ima!" said Hila. "You told me that the builders of the Babel Tower were not able to speak."

David interjected: "Why didn't they talk?"

"They didn't understand each other because they spoke different languages."

While the children were busy building the tower, Yael washed her hands and joined her sister. Devorah was silent and reflective. Unexpectedly, she started to cry. Her streaming tears stained the makeup on her face.

"Devorah, why are you crying?" asked Yael, reaching across her sister's shoulders.

"I don't know," Devorah said sobbing.

"Devorah, don't tell me you are crying for nothing. Tell me what is bothering you."

"Something terrible happened when I was a child."

"What?"

"I've never told anyone about it, not even my husband.

You know him, he would not have married me if he knew."

"Knew what?" Yael asked with anxious concern.

"Remember the days when we went to Esther's kindergarten together?

"Of course. Especially that terrible windy day; I will never forget it."

"What windy day?"

"The day you blamed me for everything, as usual," she said laughing. "That was the worst day of my life, I wanted to die."

"Well...you walked with me the first year. The second year, when you went to a different school, I went to the kindergarten all alone."

"So?" said Yael. "Is this the terrible thing that happened to you?"

"No, it happened when I was alone. I never told a soul about it."

"What happened?"

"Do you promise not to tell anyone?"

"Yes, if that's what you want."

"Well, I was raped."

After a long uncomfortable pause, Yael whispered: "Raped?"

"Yes, many times. Often, two or three times a week."

"By who?"

"He waited for me beside the kindergarten gate, took me to his shack, gave me candies and then it would happen."

"Who did this?"

"That fat Arab man who lived in the shack in the empty field not far from the *bet – mahase*."

"I don't believe it! How do you know he was Arab?"

"Father told me."

"You mean father knew about the rapes?"

"Oh, no, I never told him or Ima. I was too afraid, but he was a good friend of Abaa's."

"I never knew they were friends," said Yael. "I never saw them together. Are you sure?"

"Yes, ask Abaa."

A few weeks later, the sisters questioned their father about the fat Arab man. Enthusiastically, he said: "Oh yes, I knew him. I knew him very well. His name was Saleem. Shlomo owned the field and hired him to guard it against intruders. Saleem built a wooden shack for himself so he could keep watch. Except for Fridays and Saturdays, he was there all week. He was a devout Muslim and on Friday mornings, he went home to his wife and children in Bet – Jalla village. Sundays, at dawn, he returned with baskets full of vegetables that he sold in the Nahalat Yehudah Market. I often bought fresh vegetables and eggs from him. He is the one who helped me build the terrace on our kitchen roof; remember, we used to sleep up there on hot summer days. Your mother and I went to his younger sister's wedding in Ramala, where her husband's family lived at the time. What a wedding it was."

Yael felt the roof fall into her head. She fumed in outrage: "Abaa, what happened to this dirty, fat Saleem? Where is he now?"

"I don't know. There were rumours, either in 1946, or perhaps '47, that he raped a few girls in our neighbourhood. Shlomo immediately fired him. If I remember correctly, a Jewish family who lived near us took him to court, but in those days, as you well know, rape was not considered a crime. Later, the Israeli Secret Service discovered that Saleem's father was a close friend of the Mufti of Jerusalem. They both were deeply involved in founding, inciting and financing the Fadain Terrorist Movement. Those were stressful and aggravating times. The vicious Fadain broke into Jewish homes at night, threw grenades and killed entire innocent families."

"What happened to your friend Saleem," asked Yael sarcastically.

"During the 1948 war, many Arabs from villages around Jerusalem fled Israel. Some went to refugee camps, some to other Arab countries. Saleem and his family most probably went to Jordan where they had family."

"He was never punished?" asked Yael.

"Who?"

"Saleem."

"For what?"

"For raping our children."

"They were only rumours, never proven in court, and beside, when the British left, his file was lost."

"Abaa, what would you have done if Saleem raped your daughters?"

"This is nonsense. Saleem was a good friend. I trusted him. He would never do that."

"Abaa, let's just assume he did. What would you have done then?"

"This is silly," said Moshe. "If Saleem had dared to just touch my daughters, I would have killed him with my own hands."

To prevent Yael from inciting and upsetting her father, Devorah interrupted: "Abaa, what happened to Shlomo's field."

"Immediately after the Six Day War, Shlomo built apartment buildings on his land. He uprooted the trees, unearthed the rocks, tore down your kindergarten, levelled the Ashkenazi Batey Machase and built a beautiful modern neighbourhood. Shlomo became so rich, he took his family to America to try his luck."

"Abaa," said Yael, "it seems like this vicious cycle never ends."

"What vicious cycle?"

"We believed that after the Six Day War, all the killing and terror would stop. It doesn't look like peace is close at hand.

"One day, it will."

"When?" Yael threw the question at her father.

"When Arab priorities change."

"What do you mean, Abaa?"

"When, instead of them spending their resources and energy on destroying and terrorizing Israel, they channel everything towards education and democratization."

"Abaa," said Yael, "they claim that we are brothers, yet they stick knives in our backs; they hate us. You are very naïve. No one believes that peace between us will ever happen."

"I am certain it will, all they need to do change their rotten leaders by having a democratic election. I have the proof."

"What proof?"

"Listen to what the prophet *Isaiah* said: *And they shall beat their swords into plowshares and their spears into pruning hooks; nation will not lift sword against nation and they will no longer study warfare.*"

* * *

About 35 years later, to be exact, in the summer of 2002, Yael and her sister Devorah, with both their parents long gone, are now grandmothers, sitting again on a bench in the shade of the Yemin Moshe Windmill. They overlook the old city, still enjoying the rose blossoms and reminiscing. "Yael," said Devorah, their hands shaking, "do you remember how we sat here 35 years ago?"

"Yes I do. Nothing has changed."

"What do you mean? Many things have changed."

"Like what?"

"Remember Shlomo who went to America? Well, after the Yom Kippur War in 1973 he returned with his family.

"So what?"

"He became very much involved in the building of the new settlements around Gaza and the West Bank."

"If you consider this as a change, it is a change for the worse."

"How come?"

"Well, all those suicide bombers continue to create havoc in our lives, but what makes me really angry and sad is that the word *peace* has totally disappeared from our vocabulary."

"It seems like you lost all hope, Yael. Would you like me to recite Isaiah as our father did?"

"No, thank you. Reading without faith is meaningless. Anyway, I know it, like everyone, by heart."

"Perhaps, we need to engrave it in our minds, too."

MOTHERS

Mothers

*The stories about to be told could have happened in 1973, some-
time after the Yom Kippur War, and then 30 years later, in 2003.*

* * *

C hildren played in one of West Jerusalem's public
parks overlooking the old city; some played hide and
seek, some mothers pushed their children on the blue
swing set, while other children stood in line, waiting for their
turn to go up the yellow slide. A vibrant three-year-old girl,
dressed in red, climbed the ladder and sat on the top of the
slide, gazing at her mother for approval. Her mother
watched approvingly from an ornate black wrought iron
bench underneath the shade of an olive tree, breastfeeding
her baby. A young woman, wearing a flowery dress with
deep cleavage, sprayed water from a garden hose onto the
hot dusty plastic slide. Closer to the playground sat a woman
wearing black, and in her late 60's, alone, head fallen, tears
flowing on the open book on her lap.

A flock of greyish pigeons pecked at breadcrumbs thrown
by another lonely woman when an angry cat scared them
away. The pigeons were replaced by a flock of noisy
sparrows that dove down to have their feast, who were then
chased by a mischievous black crow.

Unexpectedly, a scream—a child's scream—rented the air.
All eyes turned to the slide. The little girl's red dress was
stuck at the top of the slide, her body hung head down,
petrified, screaming: "Ima! Ima!" The woman in black threw

her book, rushed towards the dangling girl, released her torn dress, and said with a hug: "It's okay sweetie. It's okay. Everything is alright." Panicked, the girl's mother placed the baby in his crib, and hurried to her daughter.

"She's okay, she's okay!" said the woman in black. "Except for her torn dress, nothing happened. Don't worry."

"Thank you," said the mother repeatedly while holding her crying daughter. "I don't know how to thank you. Imagine she could've fallen on her head. Thank you again...umm?"

"My name is Chana. What's yours?"

"Sarah"

"Nice to meet you, Sarah." After a pause, she continued: "What a coincidence."

"Coincidence?"

"Yes, our names both represent Biblical mothers who suffered."

"Suffered?"

"Yes. Remember Nebuchadnezzar, the King of Babylon, conquered Jerusalem and destroyed our temple in 587BC? Remember?"

"Yes, in elementary school, every child knows the story about Chana."

"Right. He forced the Jews to bow to his icons and Chana, with her seven children, refused to obey his order, so he killed them all. That's Chana's tragedy. Sarah, Abraham's wife, was a tragic character, too."

"Why? Because she gave birth to her first child Isaac, when she was 90?"

"No. She made a tragic mistake."

"A mistake?"

"Yes. Asking Hagar, with her son Ishmael, who was Abraham's son too, to leave was a sin we are paying for even today."

"I never thought about Ishmael and Isaac this way," said Sarah.

"Perhaps you could sit with me closer to the children's playground," Chana suggested. "You never know what those toddlers will do. Unpredictable, un-pre-dict-able."

"You are right," said Sarah rolling her son's crib with her daughter in her arms. At Chana's bench, she sat and fixed her daughter's dress.

Chana turned to the little girl. "What's your name?"

"Ora," she said, hiding her head in her mother's lap.

"And what's your brother's name?"

"Ori," Ora said shyly.

"Beautiful names," said Chana. "Both derive from *or*, meaning light in Hebrew.

Ora, like nothing had happened was anxious to get back to the slide. She hurried with excitement to get in line with the other children.

"Chana, are you watching over one of your grandchildren?

"No, I have no grandchildren yet. Hopefully soon. This park is my refuge. I come here often, especially when my heart is heavy and my soul feels wrinkled. Are you pregnant again, Sarah?"

"Yes. We didn't plan this one. It just happened."

"You don't want this child?"

"Of course we do, but we're in the midst of a war."

"When are you due?"

"Early summer."

"Where is your husband?"

"He is in the army, the reserve."

"Still? How come? Officially, the Yom Kippur War ended."

"They are still holding him; we don't know why. As a result, he lost his job."

"Sarah, this is against the law to fire people who are serving in the army, isn't it?"

"Yes, that's true, but he was missing for six months and his company had no choice but to replace him."

"Those wars are a disaster. Believe me, Sarah, I hate them—endless destruction and bloodshed. We need to find a way to bring them to an end."

"Do we have a choice? They surprised us on our holiest day. We only have two options: either to fight for our survival or to let them destroy us."

"There is a third option."

"What?"

"We have to make peace."

"How?"

"We need to focus our energies and resources on peace instead of wars."

"Peace could be achieved only if both sides want it. So far, we are the only ones who dream of it."

"That's not true. The Arabs want peace, too."

"Chana, that's what they say, but not what they do."

"Wars are simply no longer a solution."

"What alternatives do we have?"

"Talk. Talk with them instead of fights."

"Talk with whom? The only language they know is bloodshed and terror."

"Tell me about terror," said Chana, unexpectedly her eyes filled with tears. She pulled a Kleenex from her bag and wiped her tears silently. Sarah, wondering why she was crying, caressed her back.

"I wish I could die," mumbled Chana, in a whisper.

"Chana, come on…die!"

"Living in this country is worse than being in the concentration camps."

"How can you say that? We are finally free in our own country."

"Free? What kind of freedom is this? We aren't safe. This kind of freedom is a joke. When we came to this 'promised land,' they said: 'it is a land of milk and honey.' Milk and honey? How ironic. This land is milking our blood, devouring us alive."

"You're really angry."

"Of course I'm angry. Look, since I came to Israel, we've been through how many wars? Let's see '48, '56, '67, '73, and what about the killing in between? Have you been to our cemeteries recently?"

"No."

"Our graveyards are growing and multiplying like a poisonous mushroom field, contaminating our earth and the air we breath, blood staining our soul and mind with unbearable pain."

"Chana, how could you compare your life in this country to the Holocaust genocide in the concentration camps? This is unfair."

"Unfair!? I lost my whole family in the ghetto of Warsaw and in Auschwitz: mother, father, brothers, sisters, uncles, cousins, nephews; all of them were taken to the gas chambers. Coming to Israel with my husband, we had high hopes, dreams, expectations of being free, to live in peace, to have children, a normal family and to die in peace. Die I shall, but not in peace. Of this I am sure."

"You are so bitter."

"Yes, I am. I started a new family here and except for my daughter, they are all gone."

"Gone?"

"All killed in the wars."

"You mean our wars in Israel?"

"Yes. My husband Jacob—he was also a Holocaust survivor—I met him in Poland before the Nazis took power. We were both students in the Warsaw University. Jacob was working on his Ph.D. in Biology and I was studying Polish contemporary literature. We got married and I immediately became pregnant. When our first son Yehoshua was born, we already were forced into the Jewish ghetto. From there, we were taken to Auschwitz. I don't need to tell you what we went through there. In 1947, after a desperate effort, we finally found ourselves on a tattered, dirty, rust ridden boat headed for the shores of Palestine. By then, Yehoshua was six years old and I was pregnant again with our second child, Isaac, who I gave birth to on that boat. The British authorities, as you remember, forbad us to land in Israel, telling us to return from where we came. What did they want? For us to return to the concentration camps?

So, we were among the lucky ones. We were smuggled at night by members of the Palmach underground; they were our saviours, our angels. My husband Jacob was taken straight from the boat to an army training camp. I found myself with two children alone in a tent in a refugee camp that was strangely named Pardes - Chana.

I only saw Jacob one more time when he came to visit in Pardes - Chana. That was the only time I saw him before he was killed in 1948 while trying to free Jerusalem. I will never forget our last day together. You know what we did? Well, we only had one night, so after dinner with the boys, I sent them to our neighbours to sleep. That was a wonderful night; Jacob and I made love. He left and I never saw him again. I became pregnant with my daughter, Renana. She never knew her father."

"What happened to your boys?"

"My firstborn son, Yehoshua was killed in 1956 in the Sinai War. My son Isaac, who spent years as an army officer, was killed in the Six Day War in 1967."

"Chana, how could that have happened? The army regulations are clear: if any family member is killed in a war, his siblings are banned from the front line."

"That's what I told Isaac before he went into the army, but you know our youngsters, they have a deep sense of patriotic duty. Not only didn't he inform them about the death of his father and brother, but also insisted on being on the front line. God knows why. Perhaps he needed some kind of revenge. That's how we lose our best. In spite of that, although his death brought tragedy into my life again, I was proud of Isaac.

"What about your daughter?"

"Yes, my daughter Renana is the only surviving child I have. Thank God she is married, and ready to give birth any day. What troubles me is her husband, Amichai, who is still in the Golan Heights. I am terribly worried."

"But the war has ended, Chana. You know that. You have nothing to worry about. He will come home soon."

The soft sunrays piercing through the tree branches, joyfully played hide and seek with the children. White birds with motionless open wings glided above the soft caressing current. Two army officers entered the park gate and approached a young mother helping her son on the slide. They looked as if they were asking her a question. She pointed to Chana. Hesitantly, the officer approached her: "Are you Chana Rosenthal?"

"Yes, I am. Why?"

"We were looking for your daughter, Renana Peleg," said one of the officers.

"Her neighbour told us that she is at the hospital," said the second officer.

"We went to see her and we have good news for you," interrupted the first officer. "She gave birth to a beautiful baby boy. Your daughter asked us to tell you that you are finally a grandmother."

"A grandmother, yes, of another soldier, huh? Tell me, why were you looking for Renana?"

"We are from her husband, Amichai Peleg's unit."

"Why did you come to see me?"

"Perhaps we should go home to talk."

"We can sit and talk here. You are frightening me. Something happened?"

Both officers were obviously uncomfortable and silent. Chana turned to Sarah. "Whenever army officers come to see me, it is a bad omen, a curse." Distraught, she asked the officers: "Did something happen to Amichai?"

"Yes," answered one of the officers and as if he were anxious to get rid of something, he added: "he was wounded."

"Wounded? How? Where? When?" Their conversation sped up like a ping-pong game; it became urgent and fast.

"He stumbled on a land mine."

"Where is he? I need to see him."

"He was severely wounded."

"What do you mean, severely wounded?"

"We are sorry to tell you..."

With a fiery voice, Chana raised her hand: "Don't say anything! Don't! I don't want to hear it! He was killed. Oh God, is he is dead?"

"Yes," whispered both officers, heads bowed.

"Im-poss-ible!" shouted Chana. "Absolutely impossible!! It's a mistake. I know. Identification mistakes are quite common during war."

"Mrs. Rosenthal, we are his best friends."

"So what?"

"We moved his body to the morgue up north and we came to make the arrangements for his funeral the way you, his family, would want it. We are so…"

"No! No! No!" she said loudly, "I can't believe it! I can't take it anymore!"

"We are so very sorry. Let us take you home."

"Did you tell my daughter?"

"No."

"Why not? It's your duty."

"She was so happy with her newborn son, we thought we should wait."

Shaking knees, Chana, unstable, stood, pushed her book into her purse and quietly said: "She needs to know. I will tell her, please take me to her hospital."

"Please, Chana," said Sarah running after her, "here is my telephone number. Call me. I'm ready to do anything you need. Please call!"

Head fallen, tearlessly Chana walked with help from the two officers. She mumbled in a desperate whisper: "My little baby, my Renana, my treasure, we are all alone, facing the same terrible fate. My father, a rebel at the Warsaw Ghetto, was shot by the Germans. My husband, your father was killed as a soldier in the line of duty before you were born, your brothers too, and now your Amichai has fallen before he could see his own son.

The officers listened in silence and, after a pause, one of them simply asked: "Mrs. Rosenthal."

"Yes, my dear," she said in a heavy, black voice.

"We were told that you lost two sons in our wars."

"Yes, once I had two sons and they once had a father who

was killed in the War of Independence."

"We are sorry. We didn't know about your husband," said one of the officers.

"In our eyes, you are a hero," said the other.

"Me? Hero? This is silly. I did nothing. *They* sacrificed their lives. I would give anything to bring them back." She lowered her voice softly: "Do you have any idea, what a heavy burden—forget about it."

"I can't even imagine," said one of the officers.

"Look at the legacy that my daughter inherited; she never saw her father, and her son will never see his, except their names on a tombstone." She raised her voice: "Did you visit a graveyard recently?"

"Unfortunately, yes, many times," said one of the officers.

"So, you know. Our graveyards are growing and multiplying like a poisonous mushroom field, contaminating our earth and the air we breath, blood staining our soul and mind with...unbearable..." Chana almost fainted and the officers helped her to a bench.

"Mrs. Rosenthal, please sit down. Here are some pills to help calm you down." She swallowed the pills.

"The only thing that could calm me down," she said, "is if our leaders promise me that my grandchild will never go to war. This country is like a bird of prey devouring our people alive."

"Mrs. Rosenthal, we could arrange therapy for you."

"Me? Therapy? I don't need therapy. What we all need, as a people, is a national therapy to guide us through this Via Delorosa journey. Does anyone have any idea how?"

"Our history is our therapy."

"History...history...this reminds me what the prophet Jeremiah said about Rachel: *A voice is heard on high, wailing, bitter weeping, Rachel weeps for her children; she refuses to be consoled for her children, for they are gone.*

* * *

Thirty years later, to be exact, on a hot summer day of 2003, young veiled women, wrapped in red embroidered black garments were scattered in the field collecting wood for their cooking fire. They carried on their heads, heavy wooden bundles to their home in the refugee camp located on the outskirts of Jericho. A few of the women had babies on their backs. A group of boys played soccer on the unpaved, dusty.

Inside the camp, tightly packed on both sides of the dirt road, were stone and mud huts, wooden shacks, a few with cardboard walls, roofed with rusted tin plates. Scattered on the roofs were large heavy stones to prevent the tin from blowing away by the wind. Although the huts looked as if they were built to support each other from crumbling, they were crowded, occupied by large families. Outside, dug on both sides of the alleys were open sewer tunnels filled with stinking excrement devoured by millions of swarming, fat, silvery black flies.

A strong kick, from one of the soccer players sent the ball up swirling in the air, up, up spinning and diving straight into the sewer basin. A heavy dark cloud of humming flies rose up in anger, attacking any moving object in their path. A boy, though disgusted, pulled the ball with a wooden stick out of the sewer and ran towards the village water pump. Girls, who were collecting water at the pump, helped him wash the ball. By the time he returned with the clean ball in hand, the cloud of flies descended back onto the scum piles to continue their feast. Occasionally the boys chased away chickens, goats or sheep who crossed their playground, and continued their hot soccer game, uninterrupted.

In a blink of an eye, something terrible happened. The ball struck the goalie's head hard. All he managed to say before loosing consciousness was: *"Umi! Umi!"* Crumbled, folded, he laid on the ground. One of his friends rushed to call his

WOMEN BESIDE THE MOSQUE

mother. The others stood speechless, jolted in stillness, believing he was dead. His mother arrived, beating her head and chest, yelling: *"Ibni! Ibni! Ya – mahmudi! Ya aeni Musa."* His friends lifted him up and carried him to his hut. His enraged mother followed behind, tearing her hair, cursing Israel and the Jews who brought them all this misery.

Musa, the boy was placed on a mattress inside his hut. His mother, in her desperation to wake him up, slapped his face. Panic and chaotic commotion took over. Worrying neighbours rushed in, praying to Allah to save the boy who appeared to be dead. One of the women rushed to call the nurse from the Red Cross clinic. She came immediately.

The first thing she asked was: "Where is his father? He needs to bring him to the clinic as fast as possible. Once he's there, I'll be able to call the doctor from Jericho."

"He has no father," cried his mother.

"I'm sorry, but someone has to bring him to the clinic immediately. Please, boys, lift him carefully on the mattress and follow me."

"The clinic is too far. Why don't you call the ambulance?" one of the boys suggested.

"Our only ambulance went to the Ramalah Hospital this morning with a patient who had a heart attack. We can't wait for him to return."

"We could carry him on a donkey or on a bicycle," said another boy.

"No, no, no…he should be lying flat. Please, we are wasting time."

Musa's friends lifted and carried him on their shoulders. A procession of men, women and children gradually formed behind them, praying and pleading for Allah to help. The nurse, holding his mother's arms led the way. To distract his crying mother, the nurse asked: "What is your name?"

"Maryuma and what's yours."

"Amina. Where is your husband?"

"My husband," said Maryuma raising her hands up, "Allah protect his soul, my husband, with no work, no money, no hope, frustrated and outraged like all men in this cursed, God-forgotten camp, joined the Intafada. During one of the uprisings in Jerusalem, he was shot – dead. Some say the Israelis shot him. The Israelis say that he was shot by the Hezbalah? Does it matter who shot him now? He is dead. He left me here alone with our seven children and my sister Samira's six. Feeding thirteen mouths is not an easy task. My poor husband, would turn upside down in his grave if he knew what happened to my poor Musa."

"What happened to your sister?"

"Oh, my elder sister Samira, fell in love with Ahmed. She met him at a family wedding in the refugee camp in Janine. They got married and lived there for a few years, where their three elder children were born. They both worked in Israel: Samira as a cleaning lady with rich families in Hertzelya and Ahmed as a chef in a hotel restaurant in Netania. They managed, during those years, to save money, enough to buy a nice home in Ramalah. Their three younger were born in that house."

"Maryuma, it sounds like a success story."

"Yes Amina, until disaster fell again, like a heavy rock on our heads."

"What disaster?"

"Well, one day Israeli soldiers came to their home searching for Ahmed, but he wasn't there. They came back a few more times and never found him. Samira had no idea where he was; he simply vanished. Rumour has it that he was spying for the Israelis. The Israelis claimed that he was supporting Hezbalah terrorists. Anyway, a few weeks later, the Israelis found him in the refugee camp in Gaza. They arrested him with other men accusing them of collaborating with the Hezbalah terrorists. Amina, I swear on my mother's grave that Ahmed was never a terrorist. He was such a quiet, good boy. Only God knows the truth."

"So?"

"Well, the Israelis took him to court and found him not guilty—so they released him."

"They did?"

"Yes, Amina, he was free, but one day when Ahmed and Samira were shopping in the market, someone shot them. Ahmed died instantly and Samira died a month later in the hospital."

"Who shot them?"

"Only God knows. The Israelis say that he was found innocent and they had no reason to kill him. The Hezbalah people say that the Israelis killed him. As you can see, I had to take in their six children."

"Don't you have other family members to help?"

"I do. I have three younger sisters, but they all left."

"Left to where?"

"Well, they got married and left. One went to Saudi Arabia; one is living with her family in Baghdad and the third is in Syria. They used to send us some money, not any more. Believe me, Amina, it's very difficult to feed ten mouths."

"I thought you said thirteen?"

"I forgot to say that one day last year, my two elder sons and Samira's eldest son didn't return home. They didn't leave a note either. I went crazy. No one knew where they disappeared to. A few weeks later, someone came from Gaza with a note from them that said they volunteered to be trained for something and that they are all right. One night, on our neighbour's television screen, all of a sudden, I saw my first-born son with his body all wrapped in explosives, saying farewell before going off to commit suicide. I didn't know what to do - where to turn. I sent someone to Gaza, begging him to bring my other boys back home. I can't take it anymore, Amina. I can't."

"What happened to your first born son?"

"A few days later, his picture appeared in all the newspapers. He was the one who blew himself up beside a bus in Jerusalem. Dear Allah Rahim, why are you doing this to me?"

"And the other boys?"

"They refused to come home and asked me to send them $10,000 US. Imagine Amina, 10,000, in all my life, I've never had this kind of money."

"Why did they ask when they knew you didn't have it?"

"They knew something that I didn't know then. A few weeks after my son committed suicide, I received a check from the Palestinian authorities for $25,000 US. I was told that this was a gift from Saddam Hussein, the president of Iraq. My boys claimed that the money was to support their organization. Which organization? I don't know. They never told me."

"Did you send them the money?"

"Yes, of course, and with the rest, I bought a new TV, washing machine, fridge, stove—God bless Saddam Hussein—I also bought all of them new clothes and shoes. With the rest, I might by myself a used car. Isn't it wonderful?"

"All this is good, but still our lives, with all the killing, is hard."

"I am telling you Amina, this land is like a vulture devouring our people alive."

"I know."

"How do you know, you are not in my shoes?"

"I know. I know. The Israelis also killed my husband and my two brothers. My parents were devastated; my mother couldn't stop crying and my father could hardly speak. I was left alone, like you, with my three children."

"I'm sorry to hear that, Amina. How are you managing?"

"I'm amongst the lucky ones; I have a job. With my salary from the Red Cross and some help from my parents, I manage."

"I just wonder, when will those wars come to an end?"

"Maryuma, Never! Never! Ever!"

"Don't say that. Of course they will. They have to."

"How, Maryuma? Look at what they are doing to us. Killing us like animals in a slaughter house, destroying our homes and humiliating our leader and as if this is not enough, they named our holy city El-Kuds, Jerusalem. We will never give up this holy city, never!"

"Amina, it seems that you are forgetting something. We're killing them, too. Wars in the past 50 years have solved nothing; they prove again and again that they only add misery to our lives. The only option we have is to negotiate for peace. They recognize our right to have our own country and it's about time we recognized their rights, as well."

"Maryuma, never!"

"Have you visit our graveyards recently?"

"Oh, yes," said Amina. "Unfortunately, whenever I'm upset, I go to my husband's tombstone to talk to him."

"You probably saw that our graveyards are growing and multiplying like a poisonous mushroom field, contaminating our earth and the air we breath, blood staining our soul and mind with unbearable pain. Look Amina, they made peace with Egypt and Jordan and soon it will be our turn."

"Maryuma, you really want us to negotiate with this evil,

bloodsucking enemy?"

"Amina, demonizing each other only deepens the hatred between us and makes the situation worse. We have no choice but to respect their needs, so they will respect ours..."

"Wait, wait, Maryuma," Amina interrupted.

Finally, they reached the Red Cross Clinic. All of a sudden, Musa came to life. Sitting on the swaying mattress that rested on his friends' shoulders, he noticed the commotion of the crowd below and began to laugh—hysterically, shaking and laughing. The boys lowered him to the ground. Maryuma, elated, hurried to hug him amidst loud cheers and applause. Musa jumped off the mattress and ran to his friends, playfully calling: "Where's the ball? Where's the ball?"

Bewildered, blessing Allah for this miracle, the crowd dispersed. Amina invited Maryuma to her office for a cup of tea. They continued to share their frustration, pain and outrage. At the end of their conversation, Maryuma stood up and said: "You know what we need right now?"

"No," said Amina.

"We need therapy."

"Who? You and me?"

"No, no, we need therapy for our people—our nation. Do you have any ideas how?"

"Yes," said Amina. "I read in one of the newspapers that in Europe they succeeded in cloning human beings."

"So," said Maryuma, "what does cloning have to do with the therapy we need?"

"We need to use the cloning method to recreate all our war dead."

* * *

Three years earlier, to be exact, on July 25th, 2000 that afternoon, the sceptical international press waited outside the Camp David Peace Summit while President Bill Clinton led Ehud Barak, Yasser Arafat in negotiations. The news blackout concerning the summit was frustrating. The headlines on July 26th read:

* *Impasse at Camp David*
* *The Peace Negotiation at Camp David Collapsed*
* *The Camp David Summit Ended Yesterday Without a New Israeli-Palestinian Peace Deal. The Stumbling Issue: Jerusalem and the Refugees*

On July 27th one of the American Middle-East experts on TV said: *Yes, the negotiations collapsed but it would be premature to conclude the summit ended in failure.* Shortly after, the summit at Camp David, the Taba negotiation failed too.

What does it mean?

* * *

Victoria, an American activist in the Anti War movement, who lost her son in Viet Nam, came to a conclusion that something has to been done to stop the killing in war. Any war. In her visit to Israel in the summer of 2003, she asked Chana, Sarah, Amina and Maryuma: "What do we do now in this insolvable situation?"

"We simply don't know," they said.

"Let me tell you. We, the women, are about 50 percent of any population. As men tend to solve problems only with war, we have to find another solution. We must organize ourselves; take over power so we can turn a new page in history, which will allow us to stop all war. It is the only way to secure a stable, future for our children and generations to come. What to you think?"

Chana, Sarah, Amina and Maryuma agreed and joined her movement.

Good luck.

JEWISH QUARTER FACING THE WAILING WALL,
ON FAR LEFT: PORAT JOSEPH YESHIVA

Menahem

I don't know what to say. I have nothing to say. Nothing.
Except...well, my Hebrew name, Menahem, which
means "The Comforter," but what I really need right now
is someone to comfort me. I've lost track of time, though.
Please tell me today's date? What? Yes, of course, January
16, 2003, is a special day that will go down in history. For
over half a century, I've been watching all the events in Israel
from above, always silent. Why? Because, I didn't feel
comfortable with my stuttering, especially when I am upset;
I become inaudible then.

Today, we should rejoice and be happy. I can assure you I
won't stutter. Today, Ilan Ramon, our first Israeli astronaut is
set to ride to orbit aboard the space shuttle Columbia, an
odyssey steeped as heavily in politics and religion as in
science. His mission is to conduct a dust-monitoring
experiment designed by Tel Aviv University scientists. His
mission will be memorable for many years to come.

I hear a calling. My sixth sense tells me that I must go; my
task is to accompany the astronauts and make sure they are
safe, especially our Ilan Ramon. I'll see you soon.

* * *

Today is a disaster. I am speechless. February 1st, 2003 is a
tragic day for the world. I have nothing to say. They were all
so happy in space; they didn't want to come back to Earth.
Unfortunately, their wish became a reality. I have nothing to
say. To tell you the truth, I feel guilty that I was not able to

save them. I'm sorry, but it was out of my control. I have nothing to say. Absolutely nothing. But if you want, I can share my short story with you. You said, yes? Well, in 1947, I was in high school. The Arabs waved their flag under a heavy dark cloud of war. Military officers took all the boys in my class and me to an underground Israeli army camp. They trained us to be soldiers; we knew nothing about war, we were only kids, but we were very excited and proud to be part of our people's struggle for survival and, of course, we hoped our dream for independence would be realized. The Arab countries surrounding us—all of them—planned to invade, with intent to shave us off the face of the earth. All of them against us: Egypt, Jordan, Lebanon, Syria and even Iraq, who had no border with Israel, still joined their "party".

The British, who occupied our country at the time, knew about our training camps, but they were rarely able to find them. When they did, they took the soldiers to the gallows in Aco. The British were always on the Arab side, even refusing to accept Holocaust refugees. Imagine they didn't allow their boats to land. They didn't really give a damn. At night, we managed to smuggle in many of the homeless Holocaust survivors onto shore, providing them with food and shelter while in the midst of a raging war. What did you say? Oh, yes, this is the story, but only the beginning. Where was I? Oh, yes.

We believed then that our dream of Israel's independence would come true if we stayed faithful to our ideals. We deeply believed then, that with our solid Jewish moral foundation, our country would be the best in the world. You are laughing, huh? Well, we were naïve dreamers, yes, I agree; however, don't forget, that since 1948, while prevailing endless wars, we conquered many frontiers: we turned a barren desert to a green, lush garden; we accepted and integrated Jewish refugees from all around the world, not only from Europe and North Africa, but also almost one million from Russia and another million from surrounding oppressive Arab countries. What a boiling pot, mind you, people in Israel speak over one hundred languages. I won't digress.

Do I sound like an ancient Zionist? I don't care, I'm proud of it. Let me tell you. People tend to forget. In the past 55 years, we've conquered multiple frontiers. Take for example: agriculture, water, science, medicine, education, computers and communications; we are among the best. Take literature, for example, there is no country in the world with a population of six million people that produces as many books per year per capita. In 2001 alone, over 4,000 books were printed in Israel. This is about 10.9 books everyday of the year. Think about it. Perhaps that's why we are referred to as the People of the Book.

Our major problem now is the economy—it's on its belly—but I believe that with peace on the horizon, everything will change soon. Despite our peace with Egypt and Jordan, in reality, the killing and destruction continues to take a heavy toll. What upsets me is that hope for peace has vanished, replaced by desperation, frustration, fear and pain.

Remember the day when Anwar Saadat, president of Egypt, said during his visit to the Knesset in 1977: 'No more wars! No more wars!' Then, he sounded like an angel ringing the bells of peace. I hope that someone is listening.

I am so upset. The problem is n-n-n-o-o-o-one is lis-s-sten-n-n-n-ing. No one can hear the s-sc-cre-e-e-am-ss. of children in the d-d-a-arrrk-k-n-n-ess of h-h-h-hel-l-l-l. No one. Is the world blind? Is it deaf? Let me tell you something; the suffering of war has been burning in my heart a l-l-long time. Listen, listen to me, dear world! Is someone listening? Perhaps I should say n-n-n-othingggg. I should sssh-u-ut up, but I can't. I am so ag-g-g-ita-a-at-t-ed. Please, does anyone have some whiskey? A glass of whiskey sure would calm me down. Oh, yes, thank you, thank you very much, this whiskey is good. Where was I?

Dear World, I understand that you are upset with us Jews. I know that we have angered you for a very long time. For what? Well, today, it is the brutal repression of the Palestinian. Yesterday, it was Lebanon. Before that, it was the Six Day War followed by the War of Attrition then the Yom Kippur War and so on. All we are trying to do is simply survive. Yet, it still upsets you? By the way, did you see what is happening in Iraq now? Let me remind you what happened in 1981. The Israeli Air Force, against all odds, bombed and destroyed their nuclear reactor in Baghdad. Remember what happened then? Most countries in the United Nations condemned us. Israel, since its creation in 1948 has been at the top of the "condemnation list." Does anyone know how often we have been condemned and rejected?

Indeed, Dear World, now that we are talking about rejection and upset, perhaps I should remind you of the number of countries that have rejected the Jews: Nazi Germany, Hitler in particular, the Austrians, the Poles, the Slovaks, the Lithuanians, Ukrainians, the Russians, the Hungarians and the Romanians. This is without considering the hatred towards Israel by millions in the Arab world. Yes, I'm fully aware that many groups have unjustifiably have been rejected through the course of history: gypsies, Kurds, Armenians, North American Indians and many more. Still, if someone would assemble an Encyclopedia of Rejection, I bet the Jewish people would fill most of the volumes. So as not to upset you further, Dear World, we left to establish our own state—somewhere we used to call home—the same homeland from which we were driven out long ago. Even though we left behind the pogroms, the inquisitions, the crusades and the Holocaust, you are still upset that we repress the poor Palestinian.

In the '20's, there were no Israeli-occupied territories to impede peace between Jews and Arabs. Indeed, there was no Jewish state to upset anybody; yet, the same Palestinian slaughtered Jews in Jerusalem, Jaffa and Tsfat. Indeed, 67 Jews were slaughtered one day in Hebron in 1929. And why were hundreds of Jewish men, women and children slaughtered in Arab riots between 1936-39. Were they angry over Israeli aggression in 1967?

What happened to the U.N. Partition Plan in 1947 that proposed a Palestinian State alongside a tiny Israel? Well, the Arabs cried: "No!" and chose instead to declare war. Was that upset caused by the aggression of 1967, which happened 20 years later?

I have nothing to say. I'm so upset. There is no point. Nothing. And what about the peace negotiations in 2001 with Bill Clinton? Remember? Barak offered Arafat almost everything he wanted, on a silver platter. What did you say? You are fed up with war and politics. Well, I respect that. Perhaps, I should tell you a story that has nothing to do with war: a cornerstone in my life. A memory, a memory of a day, as a matter of fact, two days, the two days I saw her, for the first and second time. Here you are, my love, standing in front of me. I can touch your shadow.

The first time we met, my love, I was 16 years old and you were 15. We both faked our age and told the recruiters that we were 18. We volunteered for the Palmach underground and became soldiers. We found ourselves together in a first-aid course, while the war raged all over Israel. I remember the sensitive, caring way you treated a soldier whose body was punctured with grenade wounds. Strangely enough, I envied him—I wanted to feel your touch. I didn't dare speak. We were shy and timid. Your eyes were always glued to the floor and it took quite sometime for you to notice me. When you did, I was hit by lightning. Your large black eyes were unforgettable burning fire.

We were listening to the radio news, but my heart, my heart beat like a drum. It was a historic day. November 29, 1947. The radio announcer, with a shaky voice, informed us: *The United Nations General Assembly has passed a resolution calling for the establishment of a Jewish state in Eretz, Israel. The United Nations's recognition of the right of the Jewish people to establish their state is irrevocable. This right is the natural right of the Jewish people to be masters of their own fate, like all other nations, in their sovereign state.*

We were stunned; finally the world recognized our rights. Elated and happy, but still in silence, we parted, each our own separate way.

The second time we met was about six months later on May 14, 1948. I was 17 you were 16. I will never forget that day. The British Mandate over Palestine expired. The Jewish People's Council, headed by David Ben Gurion, gathered at the Tel Aviv Museum and declared the establishment of the State of Israel. Our new state was created that day. That night—what a night—God, what a night. That night you and I met for the second time. Just the memory of it gives me goose bumps. I have nothing to say. Really, nothing. I simply don't have words. Except for this appearing and disappearing image of a golden bird flying between the fluffy cotton clouds. It's an image that is still burned onto the walls of my heart; it seems like yesterday. I'm speechless. I can't talk about it. What did you say? Really? You insist on listening.

It was, well, as I said before, the evening of May 14, 1948. You were wearing your army uniform, dancing with a handsome officer. Your sweating faces shined and your eyes were glued to each other. He was holding you tight as you both flew like birds to the tune of one of Johann Strauss's waltzes. I played the trumpet as a hobby, then. I loved it. I felt like we were one when I pumped air into my trumpet. I was just a trumpet player in a military band, playing that night for the greatest celebration of our lives, a major cornerstone in our history. David Ben-Gurion, our first Prime Minister, declared that day as our first Independence Day. The whole country danced in the streets, the restaurants, in their homes, in the clubs; everybody was dancing. I wanted to dance with you. It took me some time to make up my mind and act. So, after much contemplation and hesitation, I placed my trumpet on the chair, jumped down from the stage, grabbed you from the officer's arms, and danced with you. He, of course, was unhappy, but I was elated and determined. I didn't allow anyone, including that officer to take you from me. We danced and danced—like drunken fools—we danced until dawn. Just before sunrise, we went for a walk.

Spring. Birds danced under the arched blue sky, playing with the soft sun and the gentle warm morning breeze. Spring. Fresh fragrance was everywhere. Spring. The almond trees were in full white bloom. Spring. Hand in hand, magnetically glued, we began to run. Outside the walls of Old Jerusalem—running down the mountain slope—we ran. Elated, we ran on the Judea Mountain, like children, mischievous, breathless running, passed the olive groves, over stone fences, running. We hopped through vineyards, skipped through citrus groves, and continued to run over more stone fences, running. A fresh vegetable garden, cultivated by an old farmer, stood puzzled, yelling: "Hey youngsters! Are you crazy? Did you turn mad?"

Breathless, we stood in the middle of an open field, where the soft new grass burst out of the tender soil. The field, like a woven carpet was an intoxicating symphony of wild flower colours. What a feeling. Do you remember, my love? I do. I do.

Beside the greyish rocks, the joyfully swaying cyclamen raised their pink heads on purple stems, surrounded by blood-red poppies. Wide open silky anemone petals of blue, white and red sucked in the sun's heat. An Arab shepherd, surrounded by his grazing sheep, played a sorrowful melody on his flute. We climbed up towards the mountaintop, leaving the peaceful shepherd and his herd, gently sliding down towards the valley stream. At the top of that mountain, we leaned against an old wrinkled olive tree trunk, quiet, we were still hand in hand. We drank in the view of Jerusalem, inhaling the magic image of Ancient City, hypnotized by the glorious landscape. Serenity inspired us with invisible vibrating echoes, its penetrating quiver gently infusing every cell in our body, arousing and stirring reflections of memories, not only mine, but of many in heaven, who taught me things I never knew about Jerusalem.

Dead memories. Memories buried under the earth, compressed inside and outside the walls. Invisible memories of crying and laughing, of pain and joy, torn between dreams and despair, destruction and rebirth, zealotry and hope, devastating wars and glorious triumphs, manipulated over thousands of years, by prophets, kings, empires, crusaders, religious fanatics and colonialist. Lying beneath the land, hidden memories, invisible memories, mating, seeding, coupling like lovers, copulating with enemies. Memories of admirers who built, betrayers who destroyed, mysteries, laying deep underground, memories huddled, compressed, repressed and dead under the intolerable growing weight that became too heavy to bear.

Oh, please forgive me. I've strayed again. Let's go back to what our eyes can see—the scenery we saw that day—the one that we wanted to inhale deep into our lungs, never to exhale. The sun lit the stony walls surrounding the city, embracing it with a golden hug. Like a royal crown, raising above its frame, stone houses, towers, domes and arches, sparkled like diamonds in a shimmering rainbow of colours hovering behind a silvery reddish veil over a gigantic treasury box.

After our first heavenly kiss, I picked up a red anemone and tucked it into your long black braid. Do you remember, my love? Do you remember what I whispered in your ear? I said: "Will you marry me?" You said nothing; you just stood with me. Your agile body with your apple breasts was glued to mine. Shaking and breathless, our arms paired with electricity. I lifted you up, my head between your breasts and we twirled around and around. Your legs drew an umbrella in the air around us. Swivelling like a spinning top, we kissed again, then, you whispered in my ear: "Yes, yes, yes." I was in heaven, like a gratifying dervish blessing the sublime moment. Silently, we knew. That was the happiest moment of our lives.

We walked back to our camp, making detailed plans for our future. After that day, except for when I had to join my unit for battle, we never parted. I remember what we planned on that day, May 15th, 1948. Let me remind you.

We planned too marry in May 1949, make love for the first

time as the Jewish custom requires, and be among the founders of a new kibbutz not far from Jerusalem. We were still in the army when were told that the land in the Elaa Valley was assigned to our unborn kibbutz, so we named our kibbutz Netiv Halamed Hey, after the 35 soldiers who'd been slaughtered by the Arabs at that Elaa Valley a year earlier.

We planned that in ten years, that is by May 1959, we would have a family with at least six children in our established kibbutz. 20 years after that, by 1979, our children were supposed to be married and provide us with grandchildren. By May 15, 1998 we planned to celebrate the 50th anniversary of the state of Israel and live in peace and prosperity with our neighbours. We looked forward to all this. By 1999, our grandchildren were to graduate from university, be married and provide us with great grandchildren. By then, both of us would be retired in our kibbutz, surrounded by our large family and preparing for our journey to the beyond. Those were our plans on that day, May 15, 1948.

I have nothing to say. Nothing. What? A conclusion? There is nothing to conclude, my love, and beside you asked me not talk about war. Well, you leave me no choice.

A few weeks after we became friends, still in 1948, I went with my unit, to a vicious, fierce battle against the Jordanian Legion in Latrun. The purpose of that tragic battle was to open the road leading to besieged Jerusalem. It was vital. People in Jerusalem were starving. We had no choice. Another unit tried to open the Bab El Wad Road, which we called Shar Hagai, meaning Gate to the Valley. We paid a heavy price on that day—very heavy. Thankfully, the road to Jerusalem was opened and food, water and the medication reached the people. Mission accomplished. Now, perhaps I better be silent, except I still wonder, my love, where were you that day? The day me and most of my friends were killed—dead. I would have wanted to be buried in Elaa Valley, but as our kibuttz did not exist yet, I was buried at the Mount Hertzel Cemetary. Engraved on my tombstone:

> Menahem
> Born 1931. Died 1948.
> Sacrificed his life in the battle for
> Jerusalem.

I am no longer with the living, but the image of our wedding in the Kibbutz still carries me on.

A SHEPHERD PLAYING THE FLUTE

LATRUN BATTLEFIELD

Night Song

Driving at 1:30 a.m. through the quiet streets of Jerusalem from the Hadasa Hospital to her home in the Rehavia neighbourhood, Rina felt she was riding through heaven. After 20 hours beside her daughter's bed with only half-cigarette breaks, she drove, alone, midst the heavy fog of tears and twinkling stars, feeling free in paradise. Dark clouds closed in to swallow the world, like the open jaws of a lion, and flooded it with bloody tears. Shimmering through the streetlights, reddish raindrops fell softly. God! Is it rain or blood? She remembered that she forgot to water her newly planted Bleeding Hearts. "That's the first thing I should do," Rina reminded herself.

In the far distance, she heard a gun shot, followed by the tat-tat-tat-tat-tat of an automatic weapon. Where is that coming from? Is it from Bet Jaala? Gilo or Bethlehem? She opened the radio. It blared: *all injured and fatalities were taken to the hospital.* Injured? Fatalities? Again? But where? The fragmented news was confusing. *In a hotel in Netanya.* When? *During the Passover Seder. They are cleaning the dining room after the disastrous explosion.* Explosion? What explosion? *The suicide bomber was killed with the rest.* Seder! Seder! Oh, God, it's the Seder night. Rina forgot that she was supposed to be with her parents and she didn't even call them. Rina could not take the bad news anymore and turned the radio off. She arrived home and watered her Bleeding Hearts.

2:30 a.m. Rina paced like a caged, raged lion inside her home. After this draining day, she couldn't sleep. She never thought that journal writing would alleviate her guilt—could be such a salvation. Rina felt grateful to be able to count her blessings; she can see; she can smell, taste, touch; she can walk and talk; she can sing if she wants and dance—she can even pick up a pen and write—her daughter, unconscious, paralysed, cannot. Rina wondered how to perform a miracle: how to suck her daughter's disease and pain into herself and give her back the healthy body she was born with.

Rina had faced the death of many loved ones, but none was excruciating as this. The thought that she might have to live through her own daughter's death was paralysing. She wanted to scream; she wanted to cry. She wanted to shake God and ask him simply: "Why? Why are you spilling your vengeance on my beautiful daughter? Please listen to me! Why don't you prove your magnificent glory and heal her? Please let her wake up, open her eyes. Let her move, laugh and cry. Let her walk, jump, and dance. Let her be as she used to be. Her healing is in your hands. Please God, prove to me that miracles can happen." What an irony, Rina thought. Unlike her orthodox parents, she never believed in the existence of God and now, she is turning to him? The doctors—those mighty doctors—all of them were helpless and more confused than she was. Where does she turn if not to God?

2:45 a.m. Rina called the hospital to see how her daughter is doing. The nurse told her that she is still shaking, but the tremours are less violent.

"Hold her," said Rina to the nurse. "hold her close to your body. This is the best healing there is."

Rina remembered standing frozen, speechless, unable to absorb what her daughter's neurologist had said. What did he really say? "This last relapse was so severe, I am not sure she'll make it through the night."

Confused and in total denial, Rina replied: "What do you mean?"

"Look," said the neurologist, "in my 25 years of experience treating over 1,000 M.S. patients, your daughter's last relapse was the most savage I've ever seen."

"What are you going to do to help her?"

"Well, we don't know. We simply don't know what else to do. In the past few years, we've tried everything that we know. Nothing has helped. The intravenous medication we've given her so far hasn't helped, either."

"Of course not," said Rina. "You're flooding her with poisons. Each one of you doctors sees her for a few minutes, adds another medication without knowing what the other physician did and disappears. She looks like a robot with all those tubes attached to her helpless body. Don't you see, you are poisoning her?" Rina said verging on a scream. "Her situation is getting worse every minute and you are telling me that you don't know what to do? For a start, why don't you stop all this poisoning? This madness, please! Her tremours are so violent, they're draining her, every minute she becomes weaker and weaker, she is so frail, all she needs is some peace, some tranquillity, rest, she needs to gather her strength, regain her consciousness and overcome her hallucinations!"

Quietly, the doctor said: "We only know how to deal with your daughter's situation with medication."

Rina's rage accumulated: "Pumping her body, flooding it with those medications, is simply not helping, don't you see? Please stop drowning her! *They* will kill her." Rina turned her back to the doctor to hide her tears.

The neurologist felt offended: "What do you know about medication?"

Rina turned and looked him straight in his eyes: "Doctor,

it's true. I know nothing about your medications. I can't even pronounce their names, but listen carefully to what I'm going to say. I-am-her-mother. She is part of me—my own flesh and blood. I can see and feel things that you doctors, with all your knowledge, cannot."

"Your daughter is not the only one in this hospital. We are working much above and beyond our capacity," the doctor said with little patience.

"I know, Doctor," said *Rina*, "but you have to listen to me. You said yourself that the medication does not improve her situation, so please, stop flooding her with medications."

Stumped by Rina's determination, the neurologist placed his hand on her shoulder: "This is a real tragedy. I realize that. Nothing, so far, has helped. Perhaps we should try what you are suggesting. We'll stop all the medication except for water and sugar."

Watching the nurse disconnecting the tubes, he wavered: "I suggest you to talk with your rabbi. Perhaps it would be wise if you also start making funeral arrangements."

"Are you giving up all hope for my daughter?"

"I'm afraid so," he whispered with eerie confidence, leaving Rina alone beside her daughter's bed in unbearable dread.

She simply didn't understand why the doctors—all of them—had given up on her daughter. She was always mentally and physically strong—always strong—always taking life positively. Rina knew her daughter could overcome this crisis. She truly believed she would.

3:00 a.m. The night is heavy and cold. She can't sleep. Perhaps a cup of hot tea with a lot of cognac will help.

3:30 a.m. After writing a 10-pages to God, summing up her daughter's achievements and all the reasons why she should be considered worthy of a miracle, she felt somehow relieved. Where would she turn if God wasn't listening? She called the hospital again. The nurse told Rina that her daughter is quiet now. This is a good sign, she thought. Perhaps taking her daughter off the medication had helped. Rina was so tired; she must sleep so she can replace the nurse at 7 a.m. She set the alarm clock for six; this will allow her some time for coffee and the half hour drive to the hospital.

Rina was too agitated to sleep. Her attempt to read, failed. What to do now? Pray? When did she pray last? She remembered how badly she wanted to die after a big fight with her mother when she was only ten years old. Her prayers didn't help then—thank God. The second time she prayed was when her first boyfriend went into battle in Latrun. Her prayers didn't help then, either. He was killed. She wondered if prayers will help now, yet she truly needed to pray. Her father, whenever he was under a lot of stress, sat under an olive tree at the far edge of his courtyard to isolate himself and recite Psalm 23 by King David: *God is my Shepard, I shall not lack. In lush meadows He lays me down, beside tranquil waters He leads me. He restores my soul. He leads me on paths of righteousness for His Name's sake. Though I walk in the valley overshadowed by death, I will fear no evil, for You are with me.*

Rina jumped out of her bed. She needed to see her daughter, to caress her hair, to hold her, to listen to her voice, to swallow her sadness, to give her daughter strength. She wanted to bring her back to normal.

4:00 a.m. Rina called the hospital again. The nurse told her that her daughter is sleeping peacefully—the best news in the past 24 hours—but Rina still can't sleep. Perhaps another tea with cognac. The warmth of the tea infused into a conversation she had with her daughter the day she graduated from university with almost straight As: "I'm so proud of you, Nuni. You are the best." Rina will never forget her daughter's teasing smile, the touching, challenging sparkle in her eyes. Her heart burst then with overwhelming joy. "Please God! Let me talk to her again. Let her wake up."

The dark clouds were annoying as the thunderstorm outside brewed. The banging rain on the windows drove Rina mad.

4:45 a.m. The telephone rang violently. Terrorized, Rina picked it up but, as her hands shook, the receiver fell, banging on the floor. She grabbed it: "Yes? Yes, nurse? What happened? She's awake? She wants me to come? I'm coming! I'll be there in 30 minutes. What? She wants to talk to me? Oh God! Let her talk...Hi Nuni...how are you doing? You want to sing me a song? Go ahead, Nuni, go ahead. I'm listening..." Rina, held the receiver close to her ear so that she wouldn't miss a word of her daughter's whispering voice.

In a feeble, shaking voice, her daughter sang:

To the field we went, skipping,
flowers in full bloom we found,
dancing and flower picking,
endless beauty all around.

"Nuni? You're amazing! You remember when we sang this song?"

"Yes, Ima," she responded, with renewed energy. "You used to carry me on your back like a sack of flour from the bathroom to my bedroom and dance with me. We use to sing this song together. Remember? Just before telling me stories."

"How come you remember it now?"

With a weary laugh, her daughter said: "Ima! Today is your birthday, remember? Happy birthday, Ima. I'm sorry, I haven't bought you a gift yet."

"Your call is the most precious gift you could give me."

"What?"

"Your singing, it means much more than any gift on the face of this earth."

"Really? Really, I would like to give you a hug, Ima.

"I'm coming!"

"I can't wait!"

Driving through the quiet streets of Jerusalem towards the Hadasa Hospital at 5:00 a.m. was like driving in heaven at the dawn of a new day. Scattered feathery clouds framed in gold, sailed with the wind under the ocean blue sky. Colours of soft music transformed from apricot to ruddy peach. Silvery, pink birds flew in all directions. Jerusalem at the dawn of the first Passover day is awaking. Although Rina took some classes in Arabic, she couldn't understand the Arabic letters stamped on the vegetable trucks on their way to market. Elderly groups of men, wearing their holiday dresses, were on their way to synagogues for the morning prayers. Rina, in her car, although curious about what happened in Natanyia last night, decided to keep the radio silent. She simply refused to hear about more disasters, tragedies or suicide bombers. Her focus, like a laser beam, was on her daughter. Soon she will look into her large black eyes and give her the biggest hug. As her heart beat faster, the diamond raindrops fell into one of the treasure boxes of One Thousand and One Nights. Jerusalem.

YITZHAK RABIN, MOSHE DAYAN AND UZI NARKIS
ENTERING THE OLD CITY THROUGH THE LION GATE
1967

Sound Threads

Sitting in the cool, dark theatre hall in Jerusalem, on a hot Saturday afternoon, listening to a unique piano concerto, with the reality of the Intifada all but forgotten, Ayala plays with the idea of how to portray in words, the invisible phenomenon of the sounds of music: how to describe its unifying tension and its hypnotizing power, as it magically transcends time and space; how to convey the pianist's unfolding love affair, masterfully courting the music, seducing the Jerusalem audience and, in a mysterious way, linking all in a harmonious unbroken cycle. Humbly, Ayala thinks she might try. Try, not as a music critic or a music historian, but as a storyteller—to tell a story where the principal character is the invisible—that is the music.

The cynics among us might claim that words can never capture the ineffable qualities of music. Ayala readies herself for the challenge, realizing that the only way to do so is to first cling to the visible—to what the eye can see—the music producer, the creator, that is the music player and his instrument.

The large black piano glows at centre stage, awash in a circle of yellowish lapping flames. Its large wing is raised up—wide open. From a distance, the piano looks like an enormous shiny black orchid, supported by four stem-like elegant legs, securing its existence. At times, the piano rests solidly on the floor, throwing its shadow on the shiny wooden stage, at times, like a bodybuilder, the piano legs flex their muscles, swell and lift the piano and the pianist upward, to fly, to float.

The pianist sits and hovers with the piano at the same time, one foot is in an alert position beside the piano's pedals, the other rhythmically stomping. Inseparable, both are embraced by a protective contour halo.

The pianist's cat-like torso, arching and concaving in harmonious motion, well synchronize with the reddish music's speed and splendour. In changing rhythm, his playful flexed neck leads his spinning head in various directions. At times his head rises up in frozen stillness, mouth wide open, at times, his expression flood with lust. Is it orgasmic climax or is it silent screaming pain? Is he crying out in a yellowish joy or is he in a charcoal grey agony? At times, his eyes are shut, closed, blocked in darkness, at times wide open gazing at the lucid white heights above, in deep silent prayer. Occasionally, his head slumps, thrusts down, glued to his chest, searching for refuge in his resonating ocean depths. While holding his inner energy, restraining his power from within, silently he negotiates with the oblivious spirit—his soul. Gradually he regains power, regenerating strength for the action to come. He is about to explode, to erupt, to…

In a split second his head becomes a flying butterfly, gently descending, radiating above a colourful flower field. Excited, erect, lustfully sucking the flowers' nectar, it couples with nature's creatures, deeply engaging in a divine, wordless dialogue; new motion rekindles new vibrant purple sounds, like an ascending jet plane, swept by the tides of winds. No words. Only motion and sound. Sound and motion, mirroring like a deep voice of an invisible God behind the burning bush, reflecting, invoking ever-changing feelings and visionary, fantasized images.

At various changing speeds, his shoulders rise and fall—up and down, up and down—motivating the action of responding, craving arms. Jumpy, the arms energize the pianist's agile hands. The hands trigger his flexed fingers—a pair of five-legged ballerinas—performing a euphoric pink duet. At one moment they flirt and play with the piano keys, like lovers, at the next, they vigorously fight like confronting warriors in a desperate burning blaze, a cruel fiery duel. Here, his fingers softly caress the keyboard, sliding above like a boat on the face of a calm ocean wave. Here, like a kite in the sky at increasing speeds, vibrates with the vigour of colourless winds. Here, they crawl like a heavy slow, tired, retired turtle; here like a puppet sprinter, they skip, jump, hop and run to catch up with the fleeting time.

In a blink of an eye, his fingers, with no mercy, beat the keys, forcing them to yield, to obey, to surrender. Hammering, kicking, pushing, his hands' inner energy is in total control. Now he bends toward the piano, his motionless hands sunk into the frozen keys, begging for mercy, whispering apologies, gratitude, and green blessings...

A rich palette of blue waves is followed by endless variation of blues; more blue rolling waves, whispering in blue, blowing in blue, murmuring in blue, swarming in blue. Gradually, they all wind down, fade to reflections of silvery blue flickers, uniting with marine blue ripples. The dark ripples die out, evaporating into gold-dust steam.

A new torch is rekindled, a new symphony reborn, new motions and sounds start all over again: all over again in multiple folds, new moods, new tunes, new rhythms, in endless variations of a single coloured theme. New flames ignite, spiralling into fluid white smoke, streaming, flowing vertically up, rising in veiled tubes, flowing, bowing down to be swallowed by the audience's welcoming ears.

The unbroken links invoked by the pianist and the audience beneath him, continuously intensify. This indescribable tension, that no one can see or touch, wraps the audience like invisible arms, blanketing them, restraining them in a screaming silence.

Boooom! Booom! Boom! Bom! Bom! Explosions!!! Outside, the explosions that shake the theatre walls are followed by a chain of fast ending automatic gunfire. Tik. Tik. Tik. Silence. No more explosions. No more gunfire. For a few panicked seconds, the shocked audience, erect, stood up, confused, humming: "What to do? What happened? Where should we go? Should we leave?" Some of the audience rushed to the exist doors, to find them locked and protected by security people. The lights come up. The mayhem ends when a police officer walked on stage, picks up the microphone and calmly said: "Please be seated. Sit down." The agitated audience sits. He continues: "I am very sorry about the disruption of your concert. Everything is under control."

Some of the audience interrupts: "What happened? What should we do?"

An army officer raved: "Who detonated those explosions?"

"Yes, yes," the audience requested answers.

The police officer raised his hand. Silence. "We don't know yet. It could be a single suicide bomber, it could be a group of terrorists. We are examining all options. Our first priority is to rush the wounded and the dead to the hospital, and to make sure that you are safe. In the meantime, please, for your own safety, please! Stay in your seats, continue with your concert and wait for my next announcement."

Someone lashed: "We need to go home to our children. Why don't you let us leave now?"

The police officer responded: "I fully understand, but we will let you leave only when are sure about your safety."

"Are we safe here?"

"Of course."

"How do you know? Perhaps one of the terrorists is inside here?"

Assuringly, the police officer with a deep bass, calm voice said: "This building is surrounded by our security people, so no one, including you, can leave or enter. In order to make sure that other terrorists have not penetrated the auditorium, please prepare your identification papers and soon, our policemen will check them. I hope you understand, that for security reasons, we have to do this." Loud applause.

"Are you sure there are no terrorists here?"

"I don't think so. Look around you, all the doors are secured and protected by armed policemen. You have nothing to worry about. If there is a terrorist amongst you, trust me, he will be taken care of."

The police officer steps down. Gradually, the audience sits and the pianist, too. He places his hands on the keys, waiting for the light to be dimmed. In the dark, when the audience was finally silent, he said: "I'll continue this concert from where I stopped."

The large black piano glowed at centre stage, awash in a circle of yellowish lapping flames. Its large wing is raised up—wide open. From a distance, the piano looked like an enormous shiny black orchid, supported by four stem-like elegant legs, securing its existence. Gradually, the audience is enthralled by the calming, comforting music again.

What kind of words could describe this mysterious imprisoned ecstasy, caged in a motionless trance? Visionary images come to Ayala's rescue. They begin to form, to take shape, to come to life. She can see them clearly, so vividly in her mind.

Intricate nets of silvery spider threads fill the air, stretching between the audience and the pianist, caressing all with a blessed Midas' touch. The pianist replies, responds and answers by stretching the threads, and sending them free, back to the audience. The electrified threads swell to an immense Japanese fan, ornate with butterflies, flowers and birds, circling in orbit, filling the space above. Swaying in momentum with the glorious sounds, the sounds metamorphosize. They become shiny golden ribbons gently floating, hovering, vibrating. With a lullaby melody, they peacefully sway, with a longing love song, they softly vacillate.

Instantly, in a quivering golden laser-beam, the sound, the ribbons shake in vigorous lightning tremours and gradually surrender. Then, like a vortex in a raging sea, the ribbons submerge, swallowed by the pharynx wave. Here, they revolve, roam, whirl and fade. Appear, disappear, reappear and fade. With renewed energy, they rise again, engulfing the audience, the piano and the pianist. United, the audience in the dark, inhale the threads of joy, exhale the threads of sorrow, breathe life with all its blessing. Reconciled, jointly possessed by the magical moment, a moment of release, relief, liberation. A cathartic, purifying moment, seeking and reaching a confined jubilation.

These instants of enchanting marvel unfortunately come to an end. Bewitched, drunk with god's nectar, the unrelenting audience, like a volcano erupts. Upright they stand, uprise, uproar, up. Like rebellious soldiers, they order, demand, insist: "More! More! More!" With hands clapping in thunderous applause: "More! More! More!"

Ravished, in desperation, they keep this magic moment alive, to set it still, to prolong it. A single voice raves: "B-r-a-a-v-o-o-o!" The audience's hearts, like a gigantic metronome, beat, pump in one voice: "Bravo! Bravo! Bravo!"

The distance between the pianist and the audience shrinks,

disappears, does not exist. Like an enormous peacock's ruffled feather tail, the golden shiny ribbons erect with flowers, birds and butterflies glittering above. Victorious, the audience succeeds in extending this moment to six stunning encores.

Visibly exhausted, the pianist is bowing...drained, he bows again, soaked in sweat, he bows again and again and again...Curtain down...down...down...

The pianist retreats, grabbed by the curtain's arms, swallowed in its vertically swaying mouth. The lights come up and the dream ends. Reality takes over. On stage, the police officer picks up the microphone: "Dear friends, I'd like to inform you that the explosions outside were triggered by a single suicide bomber. There are many injured and fatalities. They are already in the hospital."

"So, can we go?" said an audience member.

"Please be seated. When we open the gate, please leave quietly and slowly. If any of your cars in the parking lot are damaged, please speak with one of the policemen. We have made arrangements to take home as many as needed. Oh, the door is open."

Obstinately, the audience grabs the ribbons, holding onto them tightly, grasping, gripping, clutching, clasping. With awesome power, the ribbons pull the audience, lifting them up in the air. Intoxicated, they all fly...One by one, they vanish...One by one, absorbed by the clouds...One by one, submerged into the sunlight.

What is left behind? An uplifting glorious memory and wonder: Who was that pianist and whose music did he play?

THE KOTEL BEFORE 1947

STREET SIGN IN THE OLD CITY

Previous Titles by Esther A. Dagan

Mask: A Collection of Short Stories. ISBN 1-896371-02-7, 2002.

Emotions in Motion: Theatrical Puppets & Masks from Black Africa. ISBN 0-9693081-5-9, 1990.

African Dolls: For Play and For Magic. ISBN 0-9693081-6-7, 1990.

Tradition in Transition: Mother and Child in African Sculpture – Past and Present. ISBN 0-9693081-4-0, 1989.

When Art Shares Nature's Gift: The Calabash in Africa. ISBN 0-9693081-1-6, 1989.

Spirits Without Boundaries: 26 Single Headed Terracotta from Komaland, Ghana. ISBN 0-9693081-3-2, 1989.

Man and his Vision: The Traditional Wood Sculpture of Burkina Faso. ISBN 0-9693081-0-8, 1987.

Man at Rest: Stools and Seats from 14 African Countries. ISBN 0-920473-02-4, 1985.

Asante Stools. ISBN 0-9693081-2-4, 1988.

Dance in Africa. 58 minutes, VHS Video cassette, 1996.

The Spirit's Image: The African Masking Tradition – Evolving Continuity. ISBN 0-9693081-7-5, 1992.

Drums – The Heartbeat of Africa. ISBN 0-9693081-9-1, 1993.
Cheri Samba – The Hybridity of Art. By Bogumil Jewsiewicki. ed. Esther A. Dagan. ISBN 1-896371-00-0, 1995.

The Spirit's Dance in Africa – Evolution, Transformation and Continuity. ed. By Esther A. Dagan. 43 essays by scholars from various fields. ISBN 1-896371-01-9, 1997.

To order, please fax: 514-931-4747.